BOY WITH A BLACK ROOSTER

STEFANIE VOR SCHULTE

TRANSLATED BY ALEXANDRA ROESCH

THE
INDIGO
PRESS

THE INDIGO PRESS
50 Albemarle Street
London W1S 4BD
www.theindigopress.com

The Indigo Press Publishing Limited Reg. No. 10995574
Registered Office: Wellesley House, Duke of Wellington Avenue
Royal Arsenal, London SE18 6SS

The translation of this work was supported by a grant from the Goethe-Institut.

GOETHE
INSTITUT

Cover design © Luke Bird
Cover image © Jack Clayton
Art direction by House of Thought
Author photo: Gene Glover / © Diogenes Verlag
Typeset by Tetragon, London
Printed and bound in Great Britain by T J Books Limited, Padstow

BOY WITH A BLACK ROOSTER

1

When the painter arrives to create an altarpiece for the church Martin knows that he will leave with him at the end of winter. He will leave with him and not look back.

The villagers have been talking about the painter for a long time. Now he is here and wants to go into the church, but the key has disappeared. Henning, Seidel and Sattler – the three most influential men in the village – are on their hands and knees, scouring the rose hip bushes near the church door. The wind puffs up their shirts and trousers. Their hair is blown about their heads. They rattle at the door, again and again, taking turns, because one of them might not be doing the right kind of rattling. And each time they are baffled that it remains locked.

The painter stands next to them with his tattered belongings, watching with an amused grin. They had probably pictured him differently, but painters don't grow on trees around here. Especially during wartime.

Martin perches on the edge of the well, a mere ten paces away from the church door. He is eleven now. Very tall and thin. He lives off what he earns, but on Sundays there's nothing to be earned, so he has to fast. And yet he continues to grow. Will any of his clothes ever fit him? His trousers are always too big, and the next moment they are too small.

He has lovely eyes. It's the first thing people notice. Dark and patient. Everything about him seems calm and thoughtful. And that is what makes the villagers uncomfortable. They don't like it when someone is too spirited or too calm. They understand coarseness, deviousness too. But they don't like this thoughtfulness in the face of an eleven-year-old.

And then, of course, there is the rooster. The boy is never without it. Perched on his shoulder. Or sitting on his lap. Hidden beneath his shirt. When the creature sleeps, it looks like an old man and everyone in the village says it's the devil.

The key remains lost, but the painter is here now. So, somehow, the man must be shown the church. Henning talks in circles until he suddenly lights upon Franzi. She has the key. No one knows what prompts this notion. Still, they call for her. Martin perks up. He likes Franzi.

Franzi appears quickly. It's not far from the inn where she works. She is fourteen. She pulls her shawl around her shoulders. The wind blows her hair into her eyes. Her beauty is undeniable, prompting a dangerous desire within the men.

It turns out that Franzi has absolutely nothing to do with the key. This is annoying.

They have wasted enough time looking for it, and need to find another solution. Meanwhile, the painter has sat down next to Martin on the edge of the well. The rooster flutters off the boy's shoulder, stalks over to the painter's spattered bundles and starts pecking at them.

The three men debate whether it is acceptable to kick in a church door. Can you use force to open a house of God? Or smash a window? Which is the greater sacrilege? The door or the window? They agree that force is not good, because the only way to reach God is through faith and the Word, not through a determined kick.

'Or through death,' Franzi interjects.

How bold she is, Martin thinks. That in itself is reason enough to protect her for the rest of her life, to watch her be bold.

The painter laughs. He likes it here. He winks at Franzi. But she is not that sort of girl and doesn't wink back.

They should ask the priest, but there's only the visiting priest from the neighbouring village. They buried their own priest last year, and since then they haven't had a new one. Nor is it clear where they are supposed to get one from, because until now there has always been one, and who knows where it all started, whether the village was there first or the priest with the church. So they have been borrowing the neighbouring priest ever since. But he is no spring chicken and needs quite some time to negotiate the distance between the two villages, and so the Sunday service does not begin until past midday.

In any case, they must find out from the visiting priest how to gain entry to the church. But who should go and ask? Yellow clouds are building up in the sky, and they would have to cross the field, where there is no protection. Up here, lightning strikes every few seconds. CRACK! CRACK! CRACK! It might last all night. Henning, Seidel and Sattler are too important to the village community to be risking their lives.

'I can go,' Martin suggests. He is not afraid.

'At least in his case it wouldn't really matter,' Seidel whispers. The others hesitate. They know Martin is clever enough. He can convey the question. He will surely also manage to remember the reply. They each wrestle with their consciences and whisper among themselves. Finally, they say: 'Right then, off you go.'

'Why doesn't one of you go, in this filthy weather?' the painter asks.

'He's got the devil with him,' Henning replies. 'Nothing can touch him.'

2

The small cottage is the last one up on the hillside, where the frozen fields line the edge of the forest. You have to pass this cottage when you want to drive your cattle into the forest. Sometimes the child sits on the doorstep, greets you politely and offers his help. Sometimes the rooster perches on the handle of the grindstone, which has gradually sunk into the ground over the years and is now overgrown with lichen, immovable, hardened by frost. This is where the father sharpened his axe and then slaughtered them all, except the boy.

Perhaps it was here that it all began.

Bertram went up the hillside because the family had not come down into the village for days. They were debtors and debtors have to show their faces, so that people can hold forth about them.

So Bertram went up there to remind the family of their social obligations.

'But they were all dead,' he relates. And is happy that from now on and for evermore, everyone will be hanging on to his every word and he will always have a story to tell.

Into the cottage he went, but was immediately attacked by a black devil. The rooster. It scratched his face and hands. Bertram sought protection on his knees and only then noticed the blood.

'Blood everywhere. Stench and dead bodies. Infernal, I tell you,' he says.

'What's that?' someone asks.

'I'm saying, they have been lying there for days. The worms are at them already. A writhing mass. Yuck.'

He spits on the ground and his grandson, because he admires him, spits right alongside. Bertram pats the child's cheek.

'You're a good lad, you are.' And to the others: 'That bloody rooster. The devil incarnate. I'm not going up there again.'

'What about the boy?' someone says.

'Yes, he was alive. In the midst of it. Probably driven mad. All that blood, those wounds, gaping, you understand. You can see right into a body like that. It is not a pretty sight. The child has probably long gone mad.'

But the child was not mad and neither did he die. He must have been about three years old, and probably quite tenacious to have survived this. No one looked after him. Yes, they removed the corpses. But no one dared take on the child. Maybe they were afraid of the rooster. Possibly they were a bit lazy.

But the fact that the boy is healthy, sane and, admittedly, of a friendly disposition, is hard to fathom and difficult to accept. Some wish the child had not survived the whole thing after all – then they wouldn't need to puzzle over it and feel ashamed.

He is content with little. You can entrust the boy with your cattle the whole day, and he will accept an onion in payment. That is quite convenient. If only it weren't for the gruesome rooster on his back. This is a child born not out of love but from hunger and cold. At night he takes the rooster under the blanket, they know this for a fact. And in the mornings the child wakes the rooster, because it will sleep through the sunrise, and then the child laughs, and the people down in the village hear the laughter and cross themselves because the child is laughing with the devil and sharing his bed with him. But they continue to drive their cattle past the cottage, and have an onion on hand, just in case.

3

The alder tree in the middle of the field is engulfed in flames, then turns to black dust.

The very next lightning strike is destined for Martin. A sharp pain shoots down his back and explodes in his head. Everything stops for a moment, and Martin wonders if he might die. But shortly afterwards, or hours later, he couldn't say, he wakes up again. The thunderstorm has passed. He can still see the clouds in the sky, setting a course for else-where – they are finished for the day here.

Martin tries to get up. He has to weep a little, because he is still alive and relieved about it, but perhaps he had hoped to have put it behind him. Life. The rooster is waiting at his side.

Later, he reaches the neighbouring village and finds the priest's house. There is not a single part of his body that is still dry. His teeth are chattering.

'He is so scrawny,' the priest's wife says. 'Once we've got him out of his clothes, there will be nothing left of him.'

She wraps him in a dusty blanket and sits him down in front of the stove, where other children are already sit-ting. The priest's own. There were more of them once, but

several died. They are having porridge. The woman pre-
pares the bowls with gruel and places them on the stove.
The children push one another and hastily spit into the
bowl which they believe to contain the biggest portion, so
that no one but them will want to eat it.

They gaze at Martin in astonishment. His teeth chatter
and he tries to smile. He is not used to such cheerful children. Back home, children are always afraid. They cower
and avoid the adults, who dole out slaps. And because this
is familiar to Martin, as is the sharp pain when the leather
belt splits the skin on his naked back, he has often thought
that he is better off without a family. But a family like the
priest's – Martin would like that.

The children eat all of the gruel, but then there is also
soup. The priest's wife brings him a bowl. The soup is thin,
the smell unfamiliar, but it warms him.

He enjoys the fire. The bird has withdrawn to a corner
and hisses whenever the children come near.

Now Martin can tell them the reason for his visit. He
describes the situation in the village and conveys Henning,
Seidel and Sattler's qualms.

'What a bunch of idiots,' the priest's wife says.

The priest blinks. 'What are your thoughts on the
matter, my boy?' he asks Martin.

Martin is not used to being asked for his opinion. He has
to consider for a moment whether he has any thoughts of
his own in answer to the question.

'If God is like everyone says he is, then he won't care
whether we fetch the key or kick in the door.'

'That is a good answer,' says the priest.

'If I go back and pass on this answer, Henning won't be pleased.'

'But God will be pleased.'

'What does he know of me? There is no one who prays for me.'

'God is everywhere, and He is infinite. And He has planted some of His infiniteness in us. Infinite stupidity, for example. Infinite war.'

Martin does not feel infinite.

'We can barely contain His infiniteness. That is why it keeps escaping, and that is how God recognises us. Based on the tracks we leave. Do you understand?'

'No,' Martin said.

'Well, you…' The priest scratches his head and pulls out a few hairs. 'There, for example,' he says, and holds the hairs up. 'Our head is full of these throughout our lives, and they keep growing back. Or here.' He scratches his forearm with his fingernails until flakes of skin flutter to the ground. 'Skin,' he says in a conspiratorial voice. 'We constantly shed skin. And we need to piss. And bleed. And it never stops until we are dead. With the Almighty. But before that, He follows our tracks and finds every sinner, regardless of how well he might hide.'

The priest comes very close and plucks an eyelash from Martin's cheek with trembling fingers.

Martin looks at the eyelash. It looks just like every other eyelash, he thinks, and says so.

'But the eyelash knows that it belongs to you. And it tells God that.'

4

Now, although the priest has sent the boy on his way with some good words, he has not given him an answer that could be passed on to Henning, Sattler and Seidel. They will be dissatisfied, and obviously Martin will pay the price. Moreover, the boy is also certain that he has overlooked something. As he struggles homewards and the drenched meadows try to hold on to his feet with every step, only relinquishing them with a squelching sound, his mind is working at a level that makes his body impervious to the cold. And when he finally reaches the village, he possesses not only the knowledge of the key's whereabouts but also the appropriate response to provide to the three men.

Like the day before, the three of them are creating a ruckus in front of the church, as befits the seriousness of the situation. And although the child has shown bravery, has faced down the storm and taken the journey upon himself, the men behave as if it were Martin who owed them something and as if it wasn't they who should actually be thanking him.

'Well, look who we have here, then,' says Henning.

The painter is still, or once again, sitting on the edge of the well, eating boiled eggs that don't go down well without schnapps. Fortunately, Franzi has brought him some; Franzi, who balls her fists in her apron with pleasure when she spots the boy, Martin, whom she loves like something that only she can understand and that therefore belongs only to her.

Henning has taken up position in front of Martin. The other two follow suit.

'We can't wait to hear what you have to say,' says Seidel, and Sattler strikes the boy in the face so suddenly that he slumps to the ground.

Henning rants at Sattler: 'You idiot. I haven't even asked him yet.'

Sattler shrugs his shoulders apologetically, and Martin struggles back up. He has decided once and for all not to tell them that he knows where the key is, and also not to mention that the priest only gave confusing answers.

'Well?' Henning asks.

'Yes, well,' says Martin, licking a drop of blood from his lip. 'You must build a second door,' he says.

The three men exchange looks. It is reassuring that none of them understands.

'Into the door,' Martin says. 'Into the church door. You are to build a second door and it is to be pleasing to God in its modesty. That's what the priest said. Exactly that.'

Everyone looks towards the church door. Back at Martin. Speechless. Then at the door again.

'A modest door pleasing to God,' Martin repeats and nods. The painter sits at the edge of the well and hears everything. People are so stupid, he thinks to himself. How happy he is to have ended up here.

The three men confer, but it's no use; the priest has spoken and the men must comply. Sattler sets off to fetch tools, and soon returns with a hammer and saw. They struggle to plot the small door on the large one. They are going to need a drill.

Martin sits down on the edge of the well next to the painter, who shares a handful of nuts with him. Martin eats them gratefully, although they make his gums itch and cause the back of his throat to swell up to his ears. Franzi brings another jug of juice. They sit together while the men get to work, without much skill. Martin, Franzi and the painter experience a delicious moment of rapt contemplation, during which, for once, they need do nothing themselves and can instead observe others making a complete pig's ear of things.

The door, it is fair to say, does not turn out to be a masterpiece of craftsmanship, but Henning, Seidel and Sattler possess only moderate expertise. Their main talent probably lies in intimidating others. Which is a tried and tested method. So after sawing a rectangle into the wooden door and letting it fall into the church without applying much thought to this, they stop each other from entering, because actually, and they know this from experience, the Lord is quite strict about these things. Which in turn is not true at all. They know that too. They are probably scared of stepping through the crooked rectangle they've sawed. Their ears grow quite warm at the thought that the boy might have erred in delivering the priest's message and that they made a mistake in starting straight away instead of asking more questions. Martin's message might have turned out differently with a few additional slaps. It might have been more convenient.

Now they must organise a hinge and a lock, and as such things are not available in the village they will dismantle Hansen's front door, no, definitely not Hansen's, he is always running off, ah, right, well then, they'll dismantle old Gerti's door. She gives them a right earful, but then acquiesces when they assure her that her hinges have never been permitted to perform a more worthy task than becoming part of a church door. This, of course, will also transfer to her, Gerti. She will be allowed to use the new little door whenever she likes, because she doesn't really need a house, since the Lord is her home.

The painter grows more content to be here by the minute. He has never experienced anything quite as wonderful in all his years of wandering, nor has he encountered two such beautiful faces and honest souls as those of Franzi and Martin.

When the hole in the church door has finally become a door and, with a great deal of fiddling, the lock and key fit perfectly, Henning, Seidel and Sattler are as proud as little children. If only they had a task like this every day, then life in the village could be quite pleasant.

The modest door, pleasing to the Lord, is opened and closed and of course there is a kerfuffle about who should be allowed to go in and out first, but a brief touch of benevolence in Henning prevails and he decides that Sattler should enter the church first. Seidel will never forgive them for this. However amicably he might sit with them in the future, he will secretly be consumed by the desire for revenge, and he will make plans to get rid of them both. Poisoning, accidents – planned ones – as well as a fall down the mountain, Seidel's imagination is boundless. Seidel could consider embarking on a splendid career as a crime writer, he has so many ideas, but unfortunately his imaginings are far ahead of his time and he can neither read nor write.

Now the painter is finally called into the church.

'Do you want to come along?' he asks the child. Martin strokes the rooster between its feathers. If it could purr, it probably would.

But Martin doesn't come along, nor is he meant to, because Henning is in charge of showing the church, and the boy is one of the damned of the village and has no place in God's house.

Besides, Martin is quite tired and knows that he will see the painter more frequently now, and he is looking forward to it. Martin smiles when the dishevelled Hansen staggers towards Henning and the painter from the darkness of the church.

Yes, Martin thinks to himself, the door was a good idea. And it was also a kind of self-defence.

5

When Godel arrives, Martin is ready at once. He has slept in his clothes. He takes the rooster and places it on his shoulder.

'Does it have to come?' Godel says.

'It's coming,' the boy says.

'You are carrying the potatoes to the market.'

'Yes.'

'It would be easier without it.'

Martin smiles.

'You're going to get a hump from carrying it,' Godel says. They always have the same conversation on market days, and the boy cannot be dissuaded from bringing the creature.

They walk for a good two hours – Godel, her daughter and the boy. The trees are frozen. The landscape looks dead.

Although Godel doesn't say a word to him as they walk, and also forbids her daughter from speaking to him, Martin is still in a good mood. He likes the daughter.

He walks about ten paces behind Godel. He carries the rooster and the sack of potatoes. His wooden clogs clatter on the hard ground. His ankles stick out from his trousers; his hands from out of his sleeves. His breath comes in clouds. The rooster claws into his shoulder. Godel is holding her daughter's hand, leading a goat on her right and carrying a baby in a sling across her chest. The hem of Godel's skirt is dirty and drags across the muddy ground. Martin takes in the dragging sound until it fills his entire head.

Then he feels a rush of air – but it is only when something hits his head that suddenly it all happens: the thundering hooves of a horse, the snorting, the horseman's cloak that strikes his cheek.

In his dreams, he still feels the rush of air. The deed will haunt him from now to the end of his days.

One second, the horseman is galloping past Martin, the next he is level with Godel, lowers his hand to the girl, picks her up as if she were nothing and stuffs her beneath his cloak, this piece of darkness in the milky frost. Somewhere in this darkness is the child, who has not uttered a single cry. It all happened too quickly. Her mother's hand is still hanging in the air, feeling her daughter's warmth. And then she is gone.

The horseman has picked her like an apple; a moment later he is on the ridge. His black horse rears up.

A scream escapes from Godel. She starts running. The mewling baby swings in front of her chest. Martin runs after her, catches up, overtakes her and chases after the horseman.

The horseman. All his life Martin has known the tale of the horseman in the black cloak who snatches children.

Always a girl and a boy. And they never return. And now he has encountered him and is running after him.

The horseman in turn looks back and sees the boy with a rooster dancing around his head like a crazed shadow. The horseman shudders. He has heard about the devil in the form of a rooster. That he lives up here. He crosses himself and thinks, I have snatched a child from the devil. God Almighty! He rams his heels into the horse's sides. The horse hammers its hooves through the air. The next moment the horseman charges off, down the other side of the hill.

Martin is panting. The air tastes of blood. He falls to his knees. He knows that the girl is lost.

Godel catches up with him.

Tears are pouring down her cheeks. Martin sobs when he sees her crying. Then the rooster on his shoulder gives an ear-piercing crow. A high lament sent out into the world.

And only then does silence descend on the path.

6

The return to the village takes forever, because Godel, in her mother's grief, wavers between giving up and inevitably freezing to death at the side of the road, and pulling herself together because the infant needs her, as do the three other children who are waiting at home. Martin props up her up and helps as best he can. But when the village comes into sight Godel finally breaks down, because now she catches a glimpse of the everyday life that awaits her, when the first great period of mourning is over and she will be condemned to eternal pain. How much she will miss the little girl. The blond plait on the pillow in the mornings. The serious little face as she goes about her duties in the kitchen. But from now on, she will only sense the little girl in the corner of her eye. Like a gentle visitor from another world. She will pause for a moment in her daily chores and hope that the angel might stay, and she will barely dare to breathe. And yet the figure will fade. And each time, Godel's heart will weaken, and the pain will accompany her to her deathbed, together with the agonising question of what happened to the child.

And so Godel breaks down completely. The pain is already etched into her face and she looks years older. Tears pour down her face incessantly, and milk drips from her dress. Now she wants to lie here, oblivious to anything around her. Martin can't rouse her any more, so eventually he leans her against a tree trunk together with the infant. He hastens the rest of the way to fetch help. The boy reaches the village and shouts with what little breath he has left in his lungs after running so fast.

But because the villagers have so many misgivings about Martin, it takes an intolerably long time for them to understand the seriousness of the situation, the tale of the horseman, the calamity, and to rush down the hill, jackets flying, to help Godel. What lamentation breaks out then! They carry Godel away. Her last glance is towards Martin, and he can read it. Never again will he go to market with her. She will avoid him from now on. But perhaps he is to blame. Perhaps the black devil attracted the misfortune after all.

Exhausted, Martin stays behind at the well and rests a fair while before setting off home. The cottage on the edge of the forest, whose door has been kicked in. Although there is nothing to steal. Just a jug. The blankets and the sheaf of straw that serves as his bed.

The rooster manages to find some corn and crumbs in between the floorboards. When was the last time any baking or cooking took place here? A long time ago. Martin makes a fire, because these times call for a fire, not because he needs it. He holds his hands, frozen blue, over the embers, not because he yearns for their heat, but as an act of self-preservation.

He knows that his mind works better when he takes care of his body, at least a little. He drinks something and digs out the apple he found recently and has saved as an iron ration. He shares it with the rooster. The rooster gets the worms.

Martin chews slowly and stares into the flames. He strokes the rooster and is still awake long after the stars have come out. A whisper grips his soul; it comes from the rooster and from his own heart and becomes a decision, the gravity of which no one can take from him. The horseman; he needs to find the horseman. He will go in search of the vanished children. He uses this knowledge like a protective cloak, deep inside him. He knows now that his life has a purpose.

He falls asleep sitting up and doesn't wake until the early hours of the morning, when a terrible clattering and banging pulls the world from its night-time peace and a cart pulled by a donkey comes rumbling across the hard, frozen field at the bottom edge of the forest. A blond child is sitting on the box bashing two metal discs together.

7

Spring comes overnight. Because the weather up here is a law unto itself, it arrives quickly, and hardly anyone, not even the oldest in the village, knows what will come next. There's just a notion that things might improve. But the certainty that it will get worse almost always prevails. Hard winters turn into storms. Snow mixes with rain. Rivulets become streams. Meadows become flooded and everything turns to mud.

It is as if the fairground people brought the weather with them. Martin has never seen fairground performers before. They have tied up the donkey and propped up their cart in the area in front of the church. There is an announcement. A man, two women and the blond boy. The man has wounds and bandages; he must have been in the war. They all look exhausted, as if they have already ridden through misery and blood and have had to give a performance for death itself. Apart from the child. The child looks healthy and chubby.

They are going to perform something, but Martin doesn't really understand what. Perhaps they will portray Mary and

Joseph, the Three Wise Men or an Easter scene. Martin has not attended a service for a long time. He has no notion of holidays.

The villagers gather outside the church gate, where the cart now serves as a stage. Rain trickles down the faces of actors and audience alike. The actors deliver some laboured lines, then the little boy steps forward. Small and strong, sullen underneath his blond curls. A drip of snot swells beneath his nose. But that is forgotten as soon as he starts to sing; his voice flutters down Martin's back and makes him feel dizzy. That's how beautiful it is. The child sings as if he were running along sunbeams in the sky.

But when the child is not singing and not on his small stage, he is beastly and kicks other children, dogs and cats. He smokes and drinks warm schnapps. He is probably younger than Martin.

The child has a malicious energy that is quite foreign to Martin and interests him. He is constantly hatching pranks.

It must be down to the food, Martin thinks.

You can only come up with ideas like that if you have too much strength in your bones. And who here has that? Everyone here is glad when the day is over. No one has as much strength as this child. The village children don't play tricks on anyone. Martin marvels at the child. He is so terribly lively.

Martin wonders if other people in other places are the same and whether one day he will be able to see life somewhere, because it seems to him that everything here in the village is dead.

The village is small, and Martin encounters the child everywhere, as if he were waiting for him, as if they were destined to meet and thereby following an ancient law.

The fairground lad throws poisonous berries into the well; shoots a slingshot at the rooster and strikes it on the neck. The creature topples off Martin's shoulder, and the child laughs.

The paths are so muddy that one loses shoes and balance, and one's courage fails.

This morning, someone couldn't free his ox from the mud. The animal is still immersed up to its shoulders. From time to time, one of the children comes by and feeds the ox.

The mud only comes up to Martin's ankles, because he doesn't weigh much. He hasn't had a dry scrap of clothing on his body for days. The rooster is sick, and Martin carries it under his shirt.

He spots the child yet again. He is crouched on a wall, staring morosely into the mud. He sees Martin and immediately issues a command: 'You! Come here!' Martin doesn't really want to, but he steps closer.

'Carry me!' the child demands.

'Why?' Martin asks.

'I don't want to get wet feet,' he says.

Martin is astonished that anyone could even choose whether to have wet feet or not. He doesn't even consider the possibility of turning the child down. So he turns his back to the boy to carry him. The lad jumps onto his back and clamps on tight. Martin stumbles, because the child is much heavier than he looks, or Martin is weaker than he thought himself to be. The boy clings to him with an iron grip. Martin groans. Has he shouldered the devil? Everybody believes the rooster to be the devil himself just because of what it looks like, and the child to be an angel because he looks like one and sings like one.

Martin wonders, not for the first time, how people always know what angels look or sound like. He once asked the painter about it.

'Boy,' said the painter. 'You can be burned at the stake for questions like that.'

'But aren't angels shining lights, God's creatures and pure love?' Martin asks, because you can ask the painter questions like that. In fact, he is the only one he can talk to.

'An image of love. Don't you have an image of love?'

Martin doesn't understand.

'Your mother?' the painter asks. The boy shows no reaction.

'Siblings?'

But he has locked the memory of his siblings deep inside himself, so that he doesn't have to think of the axe that his father drove into the little ones.

The painter chews on a hunk of bread while Martin tries to identify an angel inside his head.

'Franzi,' he eventually says, quietly.

The painter grins and with a few strokes sketches Martin's solemn features on an old piece of canvas. He will carry this with him for a long time. Even long after his travels with Martin. Even then he will look at it and think that it is the best sketch he's ever done and that never again has a child stood before him so pure and unspoiled by being human. And he carries it in the pockets of his trousers, which are full of holes, until the plague takes him and he disintegrates together with the others. The piece of fabric also disintegrates; a few maggots ingest the threads and subsequently transform into a species of butterfly that no one has ever seen before and which will never exist again. And while one of the painter's pictures, a picture show-ing the boy with his rooster, will one day be exhibited in a gallery, there is – only a few metres away, in the historical museum, impaled on a wall of butterflies alongside equally dead fellow species – a butterfly that has tasted art, that has been nourished by art and that knows about the boy.

'Yes,' says the painter, knowing nothing of all this, other-wise he would give up here and now. 'Franzi is pretty. Now all your angels look like Franzi.'

The answer does not satisfy Martin. But he likes the fact that the painter has given Holy Mary, Mother of God, Franzi's features. A strong chin, an upturned nose and full lips. Martin realises that it is not really suitable, but the painter laughs and says the village deserves nothing more than to have an altarpiece that will vex them until the end of their days.

'Why?' Martin asks.

'Because of you,' the painter says. His own angels have long since assumed Martin's features.

Fiercely, he presses paint onto the palette and quickly fills in the dark areas of the altarpiece with a few cackling demons, henchmen and arrogant ogres.

Martin remembers this as he lugs the fairground lad around on his back. The child digs his heels into Martin's ribs so forcefully that they creak. The rooster squirms under Martin's shirt.

Martin is almost up to his knees in mud. The child is as heavy as lead. He pulls Martin's hair and throws himself from side to side on his back, jeering, singing and spitting. Martin groans.

The path has long ceased to be a path; it is a swamp now. Suddenly he sinks into a hole, topples over; frightened, he lets go of the manic child and smacks into the mud, which immediately fills his mouth and then swallows up the boy. Gone.

Incredulous, Martin squats in the mud and stares at the spot where the child has disappeared. He could just walk away now and no one would ask. And if someone asked, no one would believe him.

But Martin starts searching. He digs around in the damp earth and manages to grab something. It has to be the child's head. He gives a hearty tug, but something gives way and shoots towards him.

My God, thinks Martin, I've torn his head off. But no, now he sees that he is holding a skull in his hand. A head without flesh, eye sockets filled with mud, protruding teeth.

I know you, Martin thinks. He blinks, reflects and then digs his hands into the mud once more in search of the brat. This time he gets hold of him, pulls him out, falls onto his back holding him, scoops the mud out of his mouth and squeezes it out of his nostrils. And yes, there it is again, the child's horrid, endless wailing. But Martin is no longer interested in the little demon. He abandons him, takes the skull and leaves, in a strange way exultant, while the child goes on screaming. It feels as if he is holding a piece of the future in his hands. Even if he cannot guess why and how.

8

Martin enters the tavern with the skull in his hand. Henning, Seidel and Sattler are not frightened at the sight of it, but they do find the moment disconcerting. Reluctantly, they listen to Martin.

Eventually, Seidel pours water over the skull and starts wiping it down. The teeth resemble the fangs of a wild boar. Seidel shines his lantern into the empty eye sockets.

'What are you looking for in there?' Henning asks. 'Your missus?'

Everyone knows that Seidel's wife ran away. She was driven mad by all the work and the beatings from her mother-in-law. In any case, she just ran off. In the middle of the day. Threw her arms up and galloped off across the field. And didn't stop running. No one could catch up with her. They could see her running for ages, all the way to the horizon.

Seidel doesn't like hearing insinuations about his marriage. He threatens to stop serving schnapps, which quickly puts an end to the jokes.

Now the men are getting a bit spooked after all. Should they bury the skull, and is this even permitted? Does it not go against Christian principles to bury a head without a body? Which is more important anyway? The head or the body? Martin can't believe that the men want to discuss this. On the whole it seems to him that talk is all they ever do, and his gaze wanders over to the area of the bar where Franzi usually goes about wiping out the mugs and has to listen to the tales told by the old folk while their bodily odour seeps out from their shirt collars and trousers.

Franzi, whose mind is clearer than the mountain water in spring, Martin thinks. But who is damned to languish among old men who, hour after hour, recount stories from their lives while Franzi doesn't have a chance to even get to know her own life. It can't be long now until all hope inside her has decayed and is buried by this stupid chatter. These men, they know that they will soon be irrelevant, and all that remains is for them to hang themselves from the top of the roof so as not to burden their families. And if they don't manage that, because they lack courage, they will lie in their own excrement right up to the end. Tied to the bed, because the others have to work the fields or the mill, as they were once tied up as children, when their parents had to go out to the fields or the mill.

Henning, Seidel and Sattler are still talking about whether or not to bury the skull, even though they don't even know whose skull it is.

'But of course we know,' Martin says.

The men frown. They are all curious as to what the boy thinks he knows. But none of them will admit it.

'The teeth,' Martin says. 'Aren't those Wandering Ulrich's teeth?' They won't have wandered into another skull, he thinks to himself, but has long since realised that if he tries to be funny he will quickly get his ears boxed.

The men are perplexed. The boy is right. The teeth belong to Wandering Ulrich. Terrifying fangs.

He would always pass by the village on his endless travels. No one ever did him any harm. No one dared to, either, because Wandering Ulrich was always biting things in half to gain respect: a branch, a jug. Things like that. Even the wolves steered clear of him.

Now everyone is staring at the skull, as if it might say something, and everyone can now see the resemblance to the living Wandering Ulrich. The skull is cracked on one side, and someone speculates that Wandering Ulrich must have fallen. All of them have seen someone fall on his head before, how the blood – and more – comes spurting out. Some are never the same after such a blow.

Like Hansen, who fell from the hayloft and since then has been speaking with a heavy slur, but makes up for that by talking all the more. He always forgets everything but is suddenly able to play the organ. As if some abilities had squirted out of him in the fall and been replaced by others. But being able to play the organ serves him no purpose, because he is not allowed to become an organist. His spontaneous ability might be the work of the devil. So he needs to be kept away from the church. Which is not always easy.

Hansen often smacks his head against the church door in despair until it bleeds, until people can't stand it any more and allow him inside, where he sits down at the organ, bleeding and drooling, but completely happy. He plays with such fervour, and the songs spiralling out of the crooked organ are so intoxicating, it makes one want to weep. He plays and plays, but unfortunately doesn't stop, so that after the initial feeling of awe and enthusiasm, eventually a certain irritation sets in among the villagers.

Not so for Martin, who loves the organ music. But the others would prefer to return to hearing themselves talk again.

Which is why, after two days of constant playing, no one can put up with it any longer, and someone takes mercy, creeps up behind Hansen and knocks him out cold. Which is not good for his already battered skull. And which in turn means that Hansen is even crazier about the organ and perseveres even longer. A vicious circle – they know it.

Martin takes a look at Wandering Ulrich's skull, the skull he found, and says: 'He didn't fall.'

The men look at the boy.

'It needs to be examined,' Martin says.

The men exchange glances. 'What do you want to go examining him for? He's definitely dead.'

'What did he die of?' Martin asks.

'He fell,' Seidel repeats.

Martin shakes his head. 'There is a hole. Here on the side,' he says, and points to the place.

Jagged lines spread from the hole. Like when you chip a hole in frozen ice and the ice around it feels like cracking too.

The blow must have been painful. Parts of the cranium are missing.

'How do you know that?' someone asks. 'Makes no difference whether someone hit him or Ulrich fell.'

Martin insists. 'I'm sure it does.'

The men ask probing questions, and Martin prefers not to answer. He doesn't know. How is he supposed to explain that different forces probably have a different effect on the skull? He needs to prove it, so that someone believes him. He needs to prove it for the sake of having proved it.

That is the thought that grips him. He needs two skulls that are as similar as possible to one another.

He turns without another word and leaves.

9

The sky is as bright and cold as a linen sheet.

Martin walks until he senses the forest floor under his feet. He only raises his gaze once he is sure that he's surrounded by the fir trees. He has remembered where he will find two skulls.

There is this place. Everyone has heard of it, but they all avoid it nonetheless. An animal graveyard. The village has lost countless animals which, as if lured away from the herd by magic, have headed straight for this graveyard. A ravine. Around seven metres deep. They launch themselves off the edge, as if they had no sense of the danger. Or were even seeking it out. Who can say whether these sheep, goats and cattle did not die quite happy? In any case, that's how the stories go. But Martin does not know anyone who has actually been there. Neither does he know exactly which direction his steps should take, but he imagines he is on the right path and that the ravine is nearby. All noise has ceased in the forest. You have to create your own.

The rooster is restless. It's fidgeting under Martin's shirt. He takes the bird out and puts it on his shoulder. But the creature frets about there too.

'What's the matter?' Martin asks. The rooster ruffles its feathers.

Martin understands. 'It has to be done,' he says, and walks on. He squeezes through the bushes, keeping his gaze lowered, and sees animal tracks that have pierced the mantle of snow. However, they do not head every which way, as he is used to seeing them, but all in one direction like a piece of string, so the boy follows.

Eventually he steps to the edge of the ravine. At first he does not dare look down, but then does it anyway, stretches his head over the precipice. The sight is less frightening than he has anticipated. Snow and old leaves and, in between, animal bones.

As Martin looks, the rooster pushes off his shoulder and flutters a few metres away. This upsets the boy's balance for a moment, and he almost falls.

'What's the matter?' Martin asks once more.

The rooster hops around and sheds some feathers, which come to rest on the snow. It seems to be frightened. Martin stretches out his arm towards the bird, but it draws back.

'But I have to go down there,' he says. The rooster keeps its distance. 'All right,' Martin says, and his heart tightens. 'But I must fetch something. It is important.'

He hurries to find a spot that is not too steep. Eventually he chooses to descend beside a tree whose roots will help him. He thinks he can climb down hand over hand, but the ravine does not allow it. He slips at the first attempt and slithers down on the seat of his trousers. Each kick only finds the void. He is gripped by panic because it does not feel as if he is falling, but rather as if he is being pulled down. And this ravine is one that looks forward to engulfing him. What if the ground opens up and the earth swallows him?

As he topples down, everything goes black. But after one more somersault and a branch that slices a gash in his cheek, he finally lands at the bottom.

There's a high-pitched ringing in Martin's ears. Perhaps he has hit his head. Everything hurts as much as everything else. Something warm is running down his cheek. Blood from the wound.

Slowly he takes a look around. Scattered bones. Most of them bare. Remnants of fur. Rotted flesh. But above all, skeletons, skulls.

Martin struggles upright.

The sound in his head won't stop, it hums through him. Everything makes him feel strange down here. Or is it because he fell?

He manages to get to his feet and immediately stumbles again. The bones under his feet rattle and he wonders if he has ever felt a sadness like the one that is now spreading through him like toxic fumes. Does the ravine want to poison him? Will he ever get out of here? Will he ever want to get out of here? He feels sorry for the animals. He wants to grieve with them. He wants to bury them.

The people in the village say animals don't need pity. The children cuddle the cats. Now and then you look into the big eyes of a cow and wonder why they have such big eyes if there is no soul to look into.

Martin's fingers glide around among the bones. They feel the bare skulls and find two that are the same type and size. For what.

Martin has to pause. The ravine seems to be wrapping itself around him. Why is he here again? There is still something running down his cheek. But it is no longer blood, it's tears. He clutches the skulls as if they were the skulls of his lost siblings. He cries and watches himself as he feels he is about to lose his mind. And thinks about how, in a few years' time, his bare bones will be found among the animals. And someone else will wonder what happened here and what the ravine wants with all the dead. In a moment he will lie down with them and will stay there – he would do it, if it weren't for the rooster, for the rooster won't let him go.

'Martin!' he hears it call. And it is the first time he has heard it speak.

Martin has already closed his eyes but raises his head slightly.

'Come back to me, Martin. I will guide you.'

The boy nods, but his eyelids are heavy and he can't see anything.

'That doesn't matter,' the rooster says. And it explains to him how to make a pouch out of his cloak into which he can place the skulls so his hands are free for climbing. Martin follows the rooster's voice, which is gentle and melodious, but insistent and inescapable at the same time, as if a god were lending it the voice. The voice spreads through Martin as if he has been waiting for its sound all these years. It feels good to just be a boy for once, simply following the words of another creature.

And so the rooster guides him out of the sea of bones, shows him the way up the slope, points out the root and stone for each foothold and step, until the child climbs out of the sad ravine and falls to his knees in front of the rooster, exhausted.

He knows that he cannot tell anyone about how the rooster spoke to him, for they would all think it was the voice of the devil. But Martin knows that the rooster has as little to do with the devil as he himself does.

Martin is utterly exhausted. On the way home, he vomits several times; he is hot and shivery. But he does not drop the skulls or the rooster. His progress is slow, and so darkness catches up with him.

Things are grey in the transition to blackness. The skulls catch the remaining light and appear to glow. The rooster's low, mumbling voice tells him the way and drives him homewards. Tears stream down Martin's face. He wishes there were someone standing at the end of the path through the forest with a lamp, waiting for him and lighting the way.

'I am your light,' the rooster says.

Then Martin closes his eyes and blindly places one foot in front of the other. He steps over clay, stones, leaves. He hears the cracking of snail shells as he crushes them. He hears the call of an owl, the grunt of a wild boar. He does not hear the witches. Nor the undead. The rooster leads him through all the horror and superstition, but Martin does not notice and does not falter and holds the skulls left and right and reaches the village, where everything is already as dark as death.

The steps at the entrance to the village, his own footsteps on the village path, sound familiar to him; he has walked and run there a hundred times over. He opens his eyes.

Light comes from a few huts. He himself never has a light. He usually falls asleep at dusk, drowning in his exhaustion. If he can't sleep, he tries to count the stars. The rooster taught him that. But it didn't speak back then. How had it actually done that?

'There are inexplicable things in your life so that you can arrive at the explicable,' the rooster says.

Martin doesn't understand, but senses that it has something to do with the skulls. Perhaps also with the horseman.

In any case, now he enters the tavern. The men who always sit there are sitting there. Franzi is not there. She doesn't work here in the evenings. In the evenings she helps in the house, so that no one gets any funny ideas at the sight of her.

The candles flicker when Martin stumbles in. What a sight! The feverish child with the skulls and the rooster on his shoulder.

The men are startled and their eyes widen. One wets himself. But he stays seated in the puddle so that no one notices, and later pours his drink over it. Martin blinks and yearns to be back again in the solitude of the forest. He carefully places the skulls on the table, and a few thoughts run through the men's heads.

The child is very annoying, because he is so unusual and stubborn and – they don't like to admit it – quite brave, if not actually clever. All in all, entertaining. But few of them want entertaining. Most want to live in peace and quiet with their flaws.

They could offer Martin something to eat or drink, but no one thinks of that. The rooster is quiet and does not reveal that he can speak. However, the men have long forgotten that, at lunchtime, they were ranting that Martin should provide proof as to whether Wandering Ulrich had fallen or been beaten to death, as he had seemed to know the answer. Martin can't believe that the men have already forgotten about what happened at lunchtime, and it takes a while to get them back to where they were before.

And where is Wandering Ulrich's skull now? They should compare it.

No one can remember.

They search around for a bit while the feverish child sees stars dancing in front of his eyes.

Who had it last?

This place is a bloody mess.

You don't have to come here if you don't like it.

Why does Sattler stink of piss?

Shut your mouth.

Your rats are getting thinner and thinner.

Now, boy. Let's have a look, then.

Martin takes the two almost identical skulls and wraps each of them in a rag. Then he pushes the first one off the edge of the table. Next, he grabs a jug and hammers it down on the second one. The men hold their breath. Damn, what strength the scrawny fellow has! And what a gross act. Makes you think of all your own deeds where you bashed something against something else. Things that don't belong together. A child's back and a baker's shovel. Or a dog and a log. It is incredibly bothersome when a fellow keeps reminding you of these things that you have already negotiated with the Lord in devout dialogue. And then this child brings it all up again as if it were their shared conscience.

Martin unwraps the skulls from the rags and finds what he expected to see. One skull is cracked. The other has a hole. Just like Wandering Ulrich's head.

But what to do with this now? Go out looking for Wandering Ulrich's murderer even though no one is really bothered whether he is dead or still wandering? When there is a war going on and more beautiful people are dying and Wandering Ulrich would surely have ended up dead in a mountain gorge anyway, drunk as he always was, because he couldn't pull any women due to his teeth.

This also distracts from the decisive question. Whether the skull can be buried without a body and whether—

But then the child suddenly keels over and lies shivering on the ground.

Probably the fever. The boy goes into convulsions. They've seen that before with old Lisl, who is always falling down somewhere and convulsing, twitching and foaming at the mouth. They know that her convulsions are prophecies. When she goes down, the horseman comes. The horseman who steals the children.

Now that is interesting. What is it that the boy is trying to tell them? One of them thinks they should perhaps pick him up off the dirty floor, given that Seidel doesn't clean this pigsty of a place more often than once a year. But no one really wants to make the first move, and when they do make a half-hearted attempt, the black rooster jumps onto the child's chest, spreads its tatty plumage and hisses threateningly.

'Don't you touch him!' the rooster snarls. They definitely hear it.

Then the door swings open, the candle goes out, and the men let out a high-pitched scream. And are immediately embarrassed. The painter stands on the threshold and assesses the situation. He immediately registers the light, the blackness in the corners and in the men's souls. Idiotic laughter. The half-dead child with the threatening rooster on his chest. What a godforsaken village this is, and he must decorate their church.

He kneels down next to Martin; the bird allows it because it knows the painter is without malice. This fills the painter with longing, for he would also like to have such a friend, a faithful companion like the rooster. He once had a dog, but it ran away.

Martin is feverish, his eyes roll around in his head. The painter picks him up, and the rooster remains motionless on the child, who weighs almost nothing. My easel is heavier, the painter thinks to himself. He steps out of the tavern; the men stay behind, astonished. They don't know whether he is allowed to do that or not.

10

Candles illuminate the sanctuary. Scaffolding constructed from paint-splattered boards conceals the commissioned image. There are paintbrushes, paint and jugs everywhere.

The painter lays the boy down on a pew, pushes a blanket under his head, dips rags in some water and places them on the boy's forehead. The child is talking in his delirium. He raises his hands to ward off blows that he is dreaming about, of which he has had more than enough in his life. And he talks, pleads and begs of the women in the village – Gerti, Ursula, Inga – he begs for some bread, for a kind word.

The painter clenches his fists in anger. He drinks one schnapps after another as he keeps stroking Martin's hair, as if he were trying to brush the bad dreams out of the child. How the painter hates the villagers! The men are one thing. But the women! The painter is furious and spits in disgust.

There is something so wrong about the fact that the boy, who has nothing but also shouldn't have to do anything, possesses the greatest sense of decency, while the villagers make their rules and regulations on a whim, and are so content with themselves and their false lives that it's downright obscene. How they warm one another by cackling and joking, gossiping, relishing a communal wallowing in the mud like pigs. The painter knows these women, who will run to the neighbours faster than a weasel to make fun of anyone who doesn't conform, because, just like the boy, his mere existence calls their piggy-like complacency into question. They are presumptuous. They lie and cheat. They are actually stupid, but also canny, in a bad way. How is the child supposed to survive, how is morality supposed to endure between these conceited men and poisonous women? And only the child clings to the good paths, remains steadfast even when taunted, remains good even when the neighbour's watery eyes scrutinise and judge and hate him because he has seen how she keeps taking advantage all the time and everywhere while preaching modesty.

The painter drinks more schnapps and talks his visions into the boy's delirious dreams. Now and then he brings a ladle of water to Martin's lips and talks, talks himself into a rage for hours, rants and raves. At some point he jumps up and finishes the painting.

When Martin wakes up, grey light is beginning to seep into the church. He sees the canopy of black basalt of the vault above. As always, the rooster is by his side. He spots the painter snoring on a blanket.

Martin clambers off the pew. He is unsteady on his feet. Slowly, he approaches the altarpiece. Some parts are still hidden by the scaffolding, but Martin can already perceive the splendour. The heavens with golden clouds, and the tree of sorrow over there. The thieves have been moved into the distance, the boyish Jesus brought forwards.

Martin wakes the painter.

'Are you going to leave now?' he asks him.

The painter raises himself up on one elbow and is pleased that his care has helped the boy get back to health. But his head is pounding. He nods.

'Then you'll take me with you,' Martin says. The painter nods once more. Of course he'll take him. And he sits up quickly – a mistake, because now yesterday's schnapps wants out. In a moment, he feels better.

He quickly packs up his bundle and is still slower than Martin, who has nothing to pack; the rooster is always with him, and all his clothes are on his back.

Now the scaffolding. Nimbly, the painter moves hand over hand up the timbers, which bob under his weight. He needs to work quickly, because the scaffolding is only stable as long as all the boards support each other. As soon as the top one is removed, all the others want to collapse, and the painter needs to disassemble them more quickly than he can fall. He doesn't manage it without swearing, but the altarpiece is finally exposed. He kicks the last supports aside and overturns the table, quickly gathers up the colours and shoulders the stool. His glance tells Martin to move. They push the door open and leave it like that. The village is quiet. Are they really all still asleep? Martin doesn't want to say goodbye, but he would have liked to see Franzi one more time. He says as much.

'Franzi.'

Very quietly. The painter pauses.

'Not possible,' says the painter. 'She will understand,' he adds consolingly.

Martin nods. 'I will fetch her,' he says. 'I will come back and fetch her.'

The painter shrugs his shoulders and does not say that he will never return. Nor does he say that Franzi will soon be married and pregnant, and then toothless within a few more years.

He leads the way with big strides. Martin, weakened by fever, stumbles along behind him, distancing himself step by step from the place that none of his relatives has left for generations, and now he is leaving, the last of them, and it might well be that the plague carries off all the villagers tomorrow or that they kill each other; he will be elsewhere. But they won't forget him.

You might expect the villagers to be relieved that the boy with the feathered devil is finally gone and that they can have their peace. But that is not the case. When the villagers see the church with the open door, they hesitate to go in, but eventually they do, and stand in amazement. The altarpiece is finished, and they have had to wait quite a while for it.

A strip of light falls in through the church window and hits the picture at the spot where Jesus hangs on the cross, raising his head heavenwards in pain and grace. Of course, the painter has observed the effect of the light on sunny days and has arranged his portrayal of Jesus accordingly.

So they step closer, and the closer they come, the more uncomfortable the villagers feel, because in the faces – is it a coincidence? Surely not – they recognise one another.

This ugly mug here is yours.

And the nasty guard looks like you.

And then it dawns on them: Franzi is Mary, heavens, what sacrilege!

But worst of all, and no one mentions this, is Jesus. The painter has given him Martin's features. And now the child's dear face hangs in front of the villagers' noses for eternity.

11

When the painter and the boy pass themselves off as father and son, they are received more favourably.

Martin likes the notion that the painter could be his father. The painter doesn't hit him. He has not raised his voice once towards the child. Martin trusts him. The only thing he keeps to himself is that the rooster can talk.

It rains often. The wind is piercing. The painter struggles to keep his paints and papers dry. Sometimes he takes off his shirt and loden coat to wrap up his materials. Walks bare-chested. The rain runs down his shoulders. He swears and checks his bundle incessantly. Martin feels sorry for him. Even though he is just as drenched. He carries the rooster next to his skin. He carries the rooster and the painter his things. And he wonders whether the things speak to the painter as the rooster speaks to him.

The moment they reach a town, the painter grows rest-less and has to visit one of the garishly made-up women. While he lies with them, Martin guards the bundle.

Martin is fascinated by the painter's ability to capture faces, scenes and feelings in such a way that they tell the story for all time and the drawing does the remembering for him.

He too begins to draw. But the trigger is not beauty or the desire for something great. He wants no lament nor any legacy. He is interested in the scars of the war-wounded, whom they encounter in the city's alleyways and taverns.

He borrows paper and charcoal from the painter, who watches the boy struggle to draw bulging scars and incisions, empty eye sockets or the stump of an arm. The war-wounded don't mind. They get drunk and tell their stories. They like to tell the boy with the gentle eyes of their suffering. They rail about the war and grouch about the masters. They complain about the terrible food and the lumpy bodies they inhabit. There has never been enough of anything. Except for wounds, now.

'Doyouunnerstanthaboy?' they slur, and yes, Martin understands and becomes ever more absorbed in the sights and the wounds, until even the painter has had enough and drags the child out by the collar from whatever tavern they're in and searches for something pleasing, because somehow he believes he is responsible for the education of the child's heart.

But it is not that easy to find something pleasing in the midst of these foul alleys, among piss buckets, rats and rubbish. This makes the painter melancholy, because his painter's soul needs things that are pleasing.

The painter is given two new commissions. One is to paint the daughters of a draper, but they are so ugly that he has to drop the project. He is offered double his fee, the father even apologises, but the painter can't bear to look at them.

The other commission is an intimate painting for an older man. A seduction scene, set in harmless surroundings.

The painter has to find a model to train his eye for the female body. They are allowed to paint and live in the client's backyard. They are given straw sacks to sleep on. The straw is lumpy and smells of mould, but for Martin it is still a lot softer than anything he has ever known, since he has only ever slept on the floor. With nothing but a blanket and a rooster.

The painter now encounters other painters. They tell him about the young women who are willing to pose naked for a couple of coins; the women definitely prefer that to sleeping with men. But if you ask them, he is told with a wink, they won't say no either. Or you just don't listen.

Martin doesn't trust the other men. He doesn't like it when his painter drinks with the others, and later there are paints or brushes missing from the assortment. But when Martin remarks on it, the painter brushes his misgivings aside.

'But they don't want you here,' Martin says. 'They are worried that you'll take their commissions.'

'Of course,' the painter says. 'Because I am better than them.'

'You may be good enough, but you look like a pig.'

'And you can judge both?' the painter asks.

'You need to wash and get yourself a clean shirt,' Martin continues. 'Rich people like that. They stink just as much as we do, but they look clean. If you want to paint the rich more often, you need to act as if you fit in there.'

'But I don't want to paint the rich more often.'

'But then you would earn more money.'

'And what am I to do with it? I have enough to eat, drink and whore with. What would I do with more money?'

Martin is stumped for an answer. He doesn't know anything about desires that require money. He doesn't know anything about money at all. Nor about desires. He shrugs his shoulders.

'But I still don't like the others,' he mumbles quietly.

This makes the painter smile, because he realises that the child is jealous. He wants to have him for himself and look after him. He is touched.

They ask for Gloria. She is one of those willing to be painted naked. The painter sets up his studio in the back of the client's house. Martin lays out the brushes and paints for him, with sheets of paper and charcoal. Then they wait a long time for the model. And when Gloria finally arrives the room is immediately filled with her beauty and with the cries of her baby, which she carries on her hip.

The baby has its little fists buried in Gloria's hair, which is curlier than anything Martin has ever seen before. Gloria smells beguiling. The painter is pleased and scratches himself sheepishly. He loves and worships beautiful women. He becomes very polite and obliging. Gloria remains suspicious. She scrutinises Martin and the rooster. The boy cannot interpret her expression. He doesn't realise that it is just the same the other way round. No one can read Martin, with his friendly, mild gaze.

While the painter and Gloria talk, the baby stuffs its mother's curls into its mouth and chews on them. The painter counts the money into Gloria's outstretched hand. It disappears into her skirt pocket. Then she places the baby on the ground, where it sits precariously, waves its little arms around and starts to cry. Gloria slips out of her dress, picks the baby up and puts it to her breast. It drinks and smacks its lips, and the sound of the baby sucking makes Martin feel strangely content and tired. The painter immediately starts to draw them.

It is raining, but that does not bother them. They have a roof over their heads. There is work and food. The rooster sleeps in Martin's lap, Gloria hums a melody for the baby, and the charcoal scrapes across the page. The boy feels secure.

The young woman now comes every day. She increasingly entrusts the baby to Martin, who holds the little creature carefully and lets it play with his hands. Sometimes it reaches for the rooster and grabs its feathers. Then Martin has to carefully release one finger after another while the rooster curses quietly.

When Gloria poses provocatively, naked – because, after all, the painter has a job to do – Martin is embarrassed and lowers his gaze so as not to jeopardise the feeling of security he has only just found.

It seems that the painter is able to separate the two. For although he usually never misses an opportunity to talk about the merits of women, he does not utter a single lewd word towards Gloria. He does not touch her. His gaze never rests covetously on her body. He only perceives her as what she is in the context of his work.

It is clear that she appreciates it. Gloria is currently also modelling for other painters. She has to make ends meet for the baby, who is thriving and has rosy cheeks. When Gloria needs a break, the painter draws the squealing baby, who is always chasing the rooster and crawls after the creature. The way the baby tries to follow the rooster and the way the rooster furiously stalks away makes everyone laugh. Martin laughs until tears run down his cheeks. And he is surprised. He is not accustomed to this.

And then, one day, Gloria doesn't show up. They wait. It is raining outside and the light is bad, so the painter has to get the candles ready. The day passes without Gloria appearing. Martin lies awake at night and worries. The next day Gloria does not turn up at the agreed time either. They wait for several hours, then Martin goes to look for her. Perhaps she is sick. Perhaps it's the baby. But by now, Martin already suspects that something has happened.

The stench in the streets is terrible. Martin presses his sleeve over his mouth and nose. He asks for Gloria everywhere, but for a long time no one knows anything, until the boy unexpectedly steps into the centre of the misery.

'The painter's bastard!' an old woman suddenly shouts. 'Here he is.'

And they have grabbed him. A roused pack of elderly whores with an iron grip. Boys not much older than him are headbutting and kicking him. Martin is shaken; something hits him on the eyebrow. Blood trickles down his temple, and the rooster is tossed around inside his shirt as if in a storm. They drag him across the mud into a dark alley.

Martin does not put up a fight; it's obvious that they are stronger, so he has to just let it happen. His heart is pounding, not because he is scared for himself, but because he senses it is about Gloria.

Then the mob tries to squeeze through a dark entrance with him. This proves challenging because no one is willing to let go of Martin, but they can't all fit through at the same time.

Eventually some are pushed aside and stay behind, grumbling. Up a flight of stairs. The old woman pushes him up the stairs so forcefully that he barely feels the steps under his soles. She too has Gloria's wild hair; perhaps she is her mother, he thinks. There is a room. He needs a moment to understand what he is looking at.

A bed with some people kneeling by it. There is hardly any air in the room and it is very warm. Candles are burning unprotected. Martin immediately hears the baby babbling. When it sees Martin, it laughs and reaches out its little arms towards him. Jealous, a girl picks up the little one and turns it away from Martin.

Gloria is lying on the bed towards which he is now pushed. Martin recognises her by her dress and her hair, but her face carries a wound. The right cheek is disfigured by a slash, which runs swollen and flaming red from the top of her cheekbone down to her chin. Her eye above it is swollen shut and her lip is bleeding. Gloria moves her head. She has a fever and is sweating. The old woman shakes her by the shoulder and shouts at her forcefully, asking whether it was the boy who did it. Gloria opens her healthy eye, but her gaze immediately disappears again, returning to her fever dreams. Perhaps she has taken a glimpse of Martin with her.

'No,' says Martin. 'It wasn't me.'

'Then your father,' the old woman shouts in his ear. Martin shakes his head.

'Who wouldn't lie about that?' a voice says. The people make way, revealing a man sitting by the window.

Martin has seen him before and recognises him as one of the artists who welcomed them to the town in quite a friendly manner. He is a painter too. He recommended Gloria to them; he had already painted her himself. The man bares his teeth.

'But when I found Gloria, I swear to God, she called out your names.'

He seems content and quite calm. Martin hasn't trusted him since the first time they met.

'You should have killed her off properly,' the old woman hissed. 'Now she is disfigured. She won't even earn enough as a whore now. Did you take a proper look, you bastard? Have you taken a good look?'

The old woman punches Martin in the ribs and presses him down by the neck. He takes a good look. He looks at the deep cut in the face of the restless sleeper and would like to make a drawing of the gaping flesh, but of course he cannot request that. And yet the cut is nothing less than a perfect example of an angry and forceful slash with a long, thin blade. Martin can easily compare the wound with those he has copied down; the sheets of paper are in a safe place, but he doesn't actually need them any more, as he has them committed to memory. The deep cut. The clean edges. So deep that the wound won't close on its own. Not so deep as to damage the muscles underneath. Gloria will still be able to eat and speak, provided the scar doesn't get infected.

Martin looks on, and he no longer hears the old woman. And the scolding, jeering, spitting, pushing folk – who even are they? But the man at the window has some sketching materials and puts a few lines down on the paper. Probably a mourning scene. The mob at the bedside. He scrapes the charcoal over the paper, and Martin watches, and he feels as if there is only this man in the chair, and he himself has the task of seeing something. Something very simple. And then he sees it. The man is holding the charcoal with his left hand. And the wound, the high slash in Gloria's face that was carried out with anger and force from top to bottom, is on her right cheek. That can only be done by someone who grasps, reaches and does everything with his left hand.

So it was him. And not Martin's painter, who guides his paintbrush with his right hand. The rooster wriggles beneath Martin's shirt, and the boy imagines the man getting into a fight with Gloria, the shining star of this filthy gutter. Gloria, who cannot be hurt because the whores, scoundrels and poor will kill anyone who takes away the most beautiful thing they ever saw. This treasure.

Martin understands. How clever the painter was not to try and hide what he did; on the contrary, he immediately called for help. No sooner had he beaten, injured and strangled Gloria than he let go of her, shaking. Consciousness returned to his throbbing head. His mind said to blame someone else. Place yourself in the midst of the calamity and become invisible in it. Right here with Gloria, with the scolding old woman, with the angry folk; Martin realises this is where the culprit is safest.

'He has the knife,' Martin says to the old woman, who of course does not want to listen to him and instead pinches his arm.

'It must have been him,' Martin says calmly.

The old woman is not paying attention.

'He is carrying a long, narrow knife in his left pocket,' Martin says.

The old woman slowly starts to take notice. The others too stand with their mouths open.

'There must still be blood on it. He was only able to wipe it down.'

One of them goes over to the man, who clears his throat nervously and starts pushing when they come too close. But they quickly find the knife. The man is sweating, but the blade is clean.

'I can't see any blood,' the old woman says.

'The flies will find it,' says Martin.

'There are flies everywhere,' the old woman grumbles.

'Why are you even listening to him?' the man asks, and makes a move to leave. There is a tussle. He is pushed into the corner of the room. Gloria sighs in her sleep. The baby claps its hands, and everyone looks at Martin. Yes, why are they listening to him? Why does the boy make them so curious? Why don't they just wring his and the rooster's neck? And, ultimately, does it even matter who disfigured Gloria, because, since her beauty has been destroyed, the few laws that count in these alleys are also suspended? The comforting beauty. She should never have been allowed to leave the neighbourhood, then all hope would not have been lost.

The old woman thinks of the young man, the father of the baby, who asked for her hand in marriage. He was from a different neighbourhood. Wealthy, attractive and brave. He wanted to marry Gloria and go away with her. But the old woman didn't agree, because then she would lose her life insurance. Gloria made enough for everyone. So she sent the lover away, but he kept coming back and finally said very kindly that he was taking Gloria with him without the blessing of the obstinate old woman, in order to give her and the baby, which was already bulging in Gloria's belly, a nicer and above all better life. Without the old woman. Without the gutter.

That's when the old woman killed him. Stabbed him with the big scissors. Many times. He was stunned. He died stunned. Not a single scream.

She had him buried afterwards, by those who have no opinion on anything. And then the flies danced on her scissors for days. That is how the old woman knows that the boy might be right when it comes to the painter's knife.

Gloria waited for the young man for weeks and then a whole year, and couldn't understand why he didn't return, despite the old woman telling her day after day that that was just how men were. No one was ever going to liberate her from poverty. She had been born into poverty and would die in poverty, especially as she had been stupid enough to have got pregnant. Talking Gloria round had been quite tiring, and now this. All that work, for nothing.

Martin asks if the others also carry knives. No one moves until the old woman hisses an instruction. Then they come out with their knives, which may have been bought, found, inherited or stolen. Blades thin from sharpening. Some with notched handles.

They are to put them next to each other on the ground, and put the painter's knife with them. They do it, and step back into line. They cough, scuffle their feet and wait under the supervision of the old woman. The flies that constantly settle on Gloria's wound wanting to lay their eggs there are fanned away, but keep returning, again and again. But now, after they have been shooed away, they circle indecisively over the bed of the fevered woman, before finally moving away and buzzing around in the small room until they find their way to the blades on the ground. And they choose the painter's blade. Sit on it, while all the other blades remain empty.

Now of course the culprit tries to flee, but does not make it out of the door nor to the window. In any case, the fury towards him is great and his knife is returned to him several times over. Martin does not look. He just sees Gloria and he feels sorry for her.

When it is done, Martin is allowed to leave. The old woman snorts. He stumbles down the stairs and pushes the door open. He hurries to get back to his painter, and when he finally arrives, he throws himself into the painter's arms and sobs.

The painter pats his back and makes soothing noises and is happy that the boy is back. Martin is not crying because he was afraid for himself. He cries for Gloria, and because the peace and comfort of the studio is irretrievably gone. Martin recounts what happened and the painter listens to it all. Then he rubs his face for a long time, as if he were washing it, and then packs his things.

'We had better go,' he says. 'Everyone will know that you are clever, but no one will like it.'

'But the painting,' Martin says.

'That's not a painting,' the painter says. 'It's just stuff. Stuff that you get money for.'

Martin understands and does not even want to look at the presumed painting. Because he will see Gloria there. And the memory of the comfort goes hand in hand with the way she is portrayed, whole and intact.

While the painter wipes the brushes and packs away the paints, Martin draws Gloria's wound and also the knife next to it so as not to forget anything. But how could he forget?

12

It grows warmer, and the painter draws everything he comes across. Insects, plants, trees with blossoms that fall like snow from their branches. The painter sits on a stone and has Martin bring him the first beetles, which he sketches in fine detail before relinquishing them to the rooster to eat.

Martin is not very attentive. He has been jumpy and restless for days now. Spring already contains the entire death of the departing year. He sees harbingers everywhere. The trampled caterpillars. Blue around the edges, with delicate bristles, beneath which the innards spill out. The spiders' nests, from which thousands of tiny offspring scurry across last year's dry leaves. Blood in his own urine. Once, they find a dead fox with flies crawling out of its nose and maggots swarming in its abdominal cavity.

He thinks about the horseman a great deal again. Constantly keeping an eye out for a black horse, for a rider in a black cloak.

The painter, meanwhile, digs for edible roots and withered mushrooms at the edge of the forest. Martin continues to scan the sweeping hills. He lies in wait in the shadows for movement. Hoping or fearing. His heart keeps tightening.

'He's here somewhere,' he whispers to the rooster.

'Who are you talking about?' the painter asks, his head quite red from bending down so much. 'Or should I ask: who are you talking to?'

The painter is not stupid, Martin thinks. He answers the first question.

'The horseman,' Martin says.

The painter mumbles into the bark and moss of the forest.

'Don't you know the story?' Martin asks.

'Yes, I do.'

'I saw him.'

'Him?'

'Yes. His horse. I ran after him. He took a little girl.'

'From your village?'

'I have been searching for him ever since.'

The painter straightens up and bends his back so that the vertebrae crack and a fart escapes him.

'Boy,' he finally says. 'There is no horseman.'

'But I saw him.'

'But it's not just one rider. Not a single one.'

Martin is speechless. He opens and closes his mouth several times, but can't bring himself to ask for an explanation.

'How long have you known the story of the horseman?' the painter asks. Martin thinks. His whole life. 'And before you, someone else already experienced and told the story. And almost everywhere I go, someone tells me about it.

I have even painted a picture of such a rider. It is not one man, not one rider. There are lots of them.'

Martin blinks. 'And if there are lots of them, then there must be someone they are doing it for.'

The painter points at him with his earthy fingers.

'Some sort of conspiracy.'

'Does that make the search easier?' Martin asks.

'I, for one, would no longer search where everyone knows the stories.'

Martin stares at the painter. The realisation surges into his chest and fills it up completely.

'Only in a place where they don't steal children. Where they are not known. That is the only place they are untouchable.'

The painter grins and scrutinises a crooked root he is holding up to the sun. 'Yes, yes. This is a good one, and this...' He tosses a smaller one to Martin. 'You can have this one.'

Martin turns the root in his hand. It looks like a bird. He must find the rider. Find the riders. Discover the source.

'Eat,' the painter says. 'We live and eat and wander and search. And sometimes we find. Today we eat and tomorrow we move on.'

Martin nods. He is grateful. He chews the root very slowly. Gradually he calms down and thinks of the dead in his village. How some people poisoned themselves with roots. Died with a frothing stomach. They called it the *idiotic death*. There are quite a few of those: falling from a ladder and breaking your neck. Slipping in the stable and being trampled to death by the frightened animals. Missing the log while splitting wood and chopping your leg so that the blood splashes across the farm like a fountain. Or dying of poisoning.

Alongside this death there is also the *unnecessary death*, which makes everyone sigh. When children die. Or a woman's skull is smashed in after the first year of marriage. When someone is caught out by fog and falls down a slope.

But no, Martin corrects himself. In those cases the villagers spoke of a *cursed* or *sinister death*. Such a death was preceded by omens. A ghostly figure in the fog. Infants that floated above the cradle. Bleeding frogs. And Lisl, of course, who falls down in a convulsion, and who sometimes bites her tongue so badly during an episode that you can no longer understand her when she speaks.

Martin has never been able to understand the *cursed death*. He doesn't believe in ghosts and witches. And he is pretty certain that you fall into a ravine because you are drunk. And that people always talk about Lisl's convulsions when her son-in-law marches through the village in a good mood, boasting that he had a good time last night. Nothing escapes Martin's finely tuned senses. But he also knows that all the Glorias and Lisls, the Martins and the children who have disappeared have no one to stand up for them. And if you look at the dead, it is the same thing. They rest in their coffins with limbs that have to be collected from everywhere and they cannot report back.

The painter has brewed himself a foul-smelling broth from the big root, which he downs in one.

Not five minutes later, he goes into a frenzy. He tears the shirt from his body, slurs his words and jumps about enthusiastically through trees and shrubs, shouting at everything that pleases him.

He moves away quickly from Martin, who is having a hard time gathering all his belongings, shouldering the rooster and hurrying after the unhinged man.

The painter takes off at unpredictable intervals. Sometimes he lies crying in the grass and Martin catches up with him. Then, at other times, he runs down the hills so fast that the dust rises behind him, and Martin can only hope not to lose sight of him.

Only when it grows dark does the painter calm down. He waits for the stars to appear and tells Martin about them.

The boy listens to him and tries to remember the most difficult names, while the rooster pecks holes in a sheet of paper, thereby marking the position of the celestial bodies. They gaze up into the glittering darkness, into all this splendour which is not made for man, because he is supposed to be asleep at this time.

The painter seems so calm that Martin thinks the strange magic of the roots has subsided. But when the shooting stars streak across the night sky, the painter screams with excitement several times.

Eventually, however, it seems to be over. Shaking his head, the painter puts his shirt back on. Martin has handed it to him, thinking how much he likes the painter and how he would like to stay with him forever.

He is just about to tell the painter that, when he stretches and yawns and throws out the words: 'That was a truly nasty dish. The next time I am hungry, I will cook your bloody rooster!'

And that's when Martin knows that one day he will have to leave the painter. And it hurts him. The painter snores and sleeps off his hangover, while Martin stares into the night for a long time and now realises that only when you love someone do you find the path to pain and fear.

13

Everything, Martin thinks, is older than I am and has always existed. He wonders if it will ever be the other way round.

They've been travelling for a long time and have advanced far into the interior of the country. Martin feels like he is at the centre of all suffering, at the centre of those wasting away and grieving. The corpses are dripping from the trees like fermented apples. They line the fields between poppies and yarrow. The fields lie fallow. The ground is cracked and barren. Ants carry off their larvae. Martin recognises dried deer tracks in the ground. Recorded like a legacy. The forests seem to him to be full of people, but the animals have disappeared or fled this misery.

No one is speaking of the horsemen any more. Those questioned no longer have teeth in their mouths and are so thin that you would rather not ask them to speak lest they choke on their words.

When Martin asks about the horseman, he is met with uncomprehending looks.

'We are very close,' says Martin, his lips as chapped by thirst as the topsoil, and the painter shouts at him to stop wanting to save a single child, to stop chasing a myth when there is nothing around them but death and misery. All should be saved, but all are lost.

But Martin thinks differently. One saved life is all lives.

The painter says nothing. Hunger keeps him silent. Pain rummages in his intestines and turns his soul inside out. His gaze keeps falling on the rooster, which he can see, although the boy has long since taken to hiding it under his shirt at all times.

Even though Martin is constantly driven to keep on and he can hardly sleep any more because of his desire to find the horseman, he is still mindful of the painter's work. When the painter's name somehow becomes known in the miserable region, the famished man and boy receive a message out of nowhere that they must hurry to the castle of the count; a painter is needed there. The painter has a reputation that Martin did not know about until now. It is said that he can work particularly quickly. He is now given the commission to paint a family portrait.

They hurry. They are starving and hope for payment. A meal would be heavenly. When they finally reach the country estate, they look like the vagabonds that they are. They stink. Their clothes are ragged and full of bugs.

They are greeted almost effusively. The garden and palace do not seem to have heard about the misery of the world. The park is well kept; bushes and hedges bend and twist like artfully trimmed animals. As they walk along the gravel path to the main house, an excited man hurries towards them.

He introduces himself as the butler. Martin has never seen anyone with such perfect clothes and such a supple figure. He seems to be able to contort himself in all directions. Martin is completely confused by it.

The butler propels them across the gravel, chattering all the while. They enter the property through a door large enough for a church congregation. Behind this, a hallway and rooms open up, more expansive than Martin has ever seen. Empty chairs wait in corners, paintings in gold frames, candlesticks with candles burning in them even though it is daytime and no one is in the room.

The butler pushes the painter and the child into a kitchen. The large cauldrons over the fire are steaming, and Martin has to hold on to the rooster so it doesn't flee in fear. They are given bread with butter and bacon and sweet wine. The butler brings clothes and peels the painter and the boy out of their old clothes in the kitchen, as if they were potatoes in skins hardened by dirt.

'It's urgent, urgent,' he keeps saying and helps them into the unfamiliar new clothes as quickly as possible.

To his great astonishment, Martin discovers that for the first time ever he is wearing clothes that fit him. There is no need for a cord to hold up his trousers. The shoes on his feet are soft and light compared to the wooden clogs he usually wears when he is not barefoot.

The painter wears a white frilled shirt from which his dirty neck sticks out like a piece of tree bark. He seems bothered rather than pleased by the unfamiliar clothing. He burps and scratches his belly.

The butler drenches them in perfume until the bottle is empty.

'Much better,' he sighs, but the smell makes Martin feel sick. Or perhaps it is all the bread and fat. He is not used to feeling full. Perhaps it is the heat between the steaming cauldrons in which pork sides are bubbling. Martin breaks out in a sweat while the butler jumps around them as if he were everywhere at once.

Now he pushes Martin ahead of him, at the double, along the corridors. Room after room. The boy is quite dizzy from all the doors, all the possessions.

Finally they reach a spacious, elongated hall with tall windows, splendidly furnished, at the end of which sit three little people, as if they always sat only there and never had to do anything else. Martin wonders if there is dust on their shoulders, and then he has to vomit and does it on the ground in front of him. And on the butler's shoes.

Martin hears a bright laugh. Next to a rich man in a fur collar and his wife with angular features and hollow cheeks sits a girl in a stiff dress, laughing. Her mother looks at her; she immediately stops.

A servant hurries over and wipes up Martin's vomit, also running his cloth over the butler's shoe, and is angrily kicked aside.

A short conversation ensues between the rich man and the painter. They come to an agreement while Martin is still trying not to breathe in the perfume, and then the mad gallop continues – this time with the rich man, his wife and daughter in front. Martin has never experienced such a rush. And yet these rooms emanate time and ease.

But everyone is on the move. The rich girl, father and mother, the painter, the butler, Martin and the servants that follow them, they all trot silently, with rustling clothes and panting breath, through the silent corridors. Impressions pass Martin by, none of which he will be able to remember. Only the image of the running girl holding her mother's hand in front of him. The woman's hollow cheeks.

They arrive. A different room now. Wonderful light. Martin recognises a podium, like the one he has seen models pose on. In front of it, an easel, various painting materials, a canvas. The painter's stained bundle is already there.

Sweating and panting from the exertion of the unaccustomed trot, the rich man, the wife and the girl take up already agreed positions. The mother on the left. The father on the right. The girl stands in front of and apart from the mother. There is a gap between them. Someone is missing. Instead, there is a strange frame. A kind of arch and shoulder section; the frame towers at least a head above the girl.

The painter has set to work without hesitation. His instructions are gentle but direct: lower the chin, show the cheek. But the aristocrats are still out of breath, their foreheads damp with sweat.

They probably don't usually move much, Martin thinks. Then a door he hasn't noticed before opens in the wallpaper. Servants push their way in, carrying a young boy. Martin's age. He is wearing a pale blue suit. His hair is dark and straight. It keeps falling in his face, but he doesn't do anything about it. His arms hang lifelessly against his body, the tips of his feet drag across the floor.

You can see that the servants are struggling to carry the child with dignity. They could easily have shouldered him like a sack of potatoes, but the mother would probably have objected. They carry the boy over to the podium. Martin wonders if he might be wearing this child's clothes. Then the boy's head tips backwards. There is a band running under his chin and then over the top of his head. The jaw, Martin thinks, they have tied his jaw up. Then he realises the boy is dead.

But the family is looking out of the windows as if transfixed, as if they are unaware of what is happening right next to them, of how the servants wrestle with the lifeless body until they have clamped it onto the frame. The head in a semicircular contraption. Buckles that engirdle the body. Now they arrange his hair with a narrow comb. Then they carefully move away from the child. The deception is quite good. The dead boy looks normal. One hand is placed on his mother's shoulder.

She takes an audible breath. Then she says: 'He has the same eyes as his sister.' The painter nods and gets to work.

Now Martin understands the hurry. The urgency. It has to be completed before the corpse decays. Before they all lose their minds. Now the hours pass. Perfume is sprayed around the room from time to time. The dead boy's hand keeps slipping off his mother's shoulder. At first, servants jump in, but later Martin takes over the task. He finds he doesn't mind much. While he does it, he discovers a mark on the boy's neck, a red ring running around his neck. He knows it is the trace of a rope; he has seen it before, on Farmer Wittel, whom he discovered in the woods. No one gave a damn. Seidel said he hanged himself because he couldn't find his balls in his trousers.

Hours pass. Wine, bread and cheese are brought for the painter. Servants feed the family with pieces of cake. They brush crumbs from their collars and annoying flies from their noses, and bring them spoonfuls of water.

When daylight fades, candlesticks are brought in. Hundreds of candles now illuminate the easel and the family group. A leaden warmth suffocates the air. The sitters' eyes keep drooping shut. The girl has sat down and is leaning against her mother. Martin also keeps falling asleep, then wakes up startled and pulls himself up, but he hears and sees the painter working, which calms him and sends him back to sleep.

But at some point it stops. Then the silence wakes him.

The rich girl is now sleeping stretched out on the podium; her mother's chin has sunk to her chest. The father is snoring. The dead boy looks the most alive. His skin shimmers. The shadow play makes you think he is moving, breathing, perhaps smiling and winking at Martin. He presses the rooster close. He wants to get up and look at the painting. The painter is resting in his chair, his arms crossed in front of his chest.

The wallpaper door opens quietly. As so often that evening, one of the countless servants – who are all dressed identically, who are all of similar stature and height, not noticeably different, which is why they were chosen – appears. He tiptoes in, just this one, and he has taken off his shoes.

Martin does not move and closes his eyes. He opens them again when he senses that the servant is no longer nearby. The man is whispering to himself. It sounds hurried, vengeful and mad. He takes one of the candlesticks, turns towards the windows and, without hesitating, holds the flames against the curtains.

The flames immediately eat their way up towards the ceiling. The servant is already at the next window and the one after that and has made the rounds so quickly that Martin hardly has time to scream. And yet he does. And the man hears him.

With sweeping steps the servant rushes across the hall. He runs towards Martin as if possessed and chokes out a sound; Martin has never heard anything more terrible. The man reaches out his arms towards Martin.

He's going to kill me, Martin thinks, stuck inside his own body as though in a suit of armour.

But then the rooster launches himself between them, opens its beak and gives an ear-piercing screech. It shrieks and pecks at the servant, who immediately turns and, before anyone can react, disappears through the wallpaper door. Other servants immediately pour in and no one can tell any more whether the arsonist is among them or has fled.

Meanwhile, those sleeping awaken slowly and feebly amid the heat of the flames and the crackling.

The father picks up the little girl, while the mother tries to release the dead boy from his restraints. But the buckles refuse to be opened. She tugs at her dead child until she has to give up. Meanwhile, two servants rescue the painting. Chaos ensues. Buckets of water are thrown against the wall of flames, but no one really knows where to go first, and no one is in charge. The identical servants end up spinning around in an ineffectual ballet between smoke, hissing flames and puddles of water.

A light wind spreads the spraying sparks throughout the entire property. After less than an hour, there is no more hope.

Everyone is outside, blackened with soot and exhausted. They gaze mutely at the blazing structure from the large lawn. The rich are no longer rich. They are just as filthy as the servants, who leave the garden one after the other. They shuffle away. They throw their wigs into the hedge and take off their tight jackets. The tutors leave. The cooks. The carriage drivers. The butler is the last to go. The little girl cries at the sight of the destroyed home.

'You can come with us,' Martin says to her. But their gaze only briefly rests on his face.

'Come,' the painter says. 'There is nothing more to do here.'

When Martin looks back one last time, the three of them are still standing there. They hold the painting between them and watch the walls come tumbling down.

14

At night it is dark only for a short time until morning dawns again. The sky is always pink and the days grow hot. Each one hotter than the one before.

They often suffer from hunger. The thirst is worse. There is war everywhere and no one needs a painting.

'Which doesn't mean that none should be done,' says the painter, and uses the colours he has left to paint on the paper he has left. Eventually all the sheets are used up. He continues to paint on wood, on stone, and then he runs out of colours. First blue, then yellow. In the end, the paintings are all red, and then nothing at all. The painter has used up all his materials.

'Now I have nothing,' he says, and looks into space.

'Can we get more paint?' Martin asks.

'There probably is some. Somewhere.'

'Then we will get you what you need.'

The painter says nothing.

They stay away from the cities but keep coming across homeless people in the forests, wandering among the dry trees just as they are. One time they meet a mother and daughter. The mother seems half-dead with fear. She keeps asking for a knife. It takes them a long time to find out what the woman wants. Only then do they give it to her and look on as she cuts her daughter's hair. She begs Martin to give her his trousers so that the girl will look like a boy and perhaps be spared the worst.

'That is for me to bear,' she says.

The painter says nothing.

'Please,' the mother begs Martin. Tears stream down her cheeks, but her face does not cry. The sadness just pours out of her as if there were no end to it. Where might her husband and the other children be?

The dead are everywhere. They lie in the bushes, one finds them like one finds berries. They are piled up in the towns and burned. Martin knows that he will find other trousers. He gives them to the girl.

This thirst. The painter swears a lot and claims that's the reason. But it's because he can't find work as a painter, Martin is sure of it. Soon the painter no longer speaks to the child. He trudges silently through the dry woods and across the parched fields teeming with potato beetles, which shred everything that remains. He no longer pays attention to whether Martin is keeping up.

Martin has to keep the rooster constantly hidden all the time. Everyone who crosses their path has hollow cheeks and fever-glazed eyes. They would kill one another to eat the rooster. Why don't they just eat one another? They probably already do.

The terrible days erode all love, patience and care between the painter and the boy. The trust is ebbing away. More and more often, Martin gets a fright when the painter appears silently behind him and stares dully at him and the creature on his lap. One night Martin wakes up and the painter is standing over him, his head with the tangled hair floating like black doom against the starry sky. He is holding a heavy stone in one hand.

'What are you doing?' Martin whispers fearfully.

He hears the painter grind his teeth.

'What are you doing?' he asks again.

But it may be that he didn't say it again, because his heart is beating so fast that he can't hear himself speak.

This shocks the painter out of his paralysis. He runs off, runs into the nearest bushes, tearing and cracking through the branches. And Martin also jumps up and runs off in the other direction, away from the painter whom he loves.

He has seen the superhuman effort it took the painter not to bash in his and the rooster's head. Not yet.

So Martin must get away from him.

He runs until he coughs up blood. And he runs until he can't think any more.

15

Martin finds a river and, on the bank, a boat. There is only one oar, but he knows nothing about rowing. He can't swim either; he knows nothing about rivers or currents.

He hesitates before he gets in the boat. But an unmistakable sound from the forest strengthens his resolve. The rooster has heard it too. People.

Martin pushes the boat away from the bank and lies down inside it.

Trees glide into his line of vision. He sees leaves glistening in the sun and tries to forget the corpses rotting in the forests and withering in the fields. He no longer wants to think about the gnawed bones of horses, the thirsty children, the violated women and the mutilated men.

He holds the rooster tight and lets himself drift down the river. The painter once told him that all rivers want to reach the sea but not all of them make it. He has seen the sea in paintings. Stormy seas in rich people's paintings. Grey water. Then blue and smooth. White birds on it. Boats and people.

'Rooster,' Martin says. He is so exhausted and tired. He does not need to say that he is afraid.

'You need to keep looking,' the rooster says.

'The task is too great.'

'The task entered the world with you and now it fits you like a glove.'

'Who put it in my cradle?'

'You didn't have a cradle. And you were always crying. You probably already knew your fate. Or that of the others.'

'Tell me,' Martin says.

'How they loved you!' the rooster said. 'They carried you all the time. No thought of hurting you.'

Martin has always believed that he was entirely without love. Even though there may be an image in his memory of his father in which the man was not carrying out the deed. But that image stands, immovable, blocking all other memories. The raised axe and the distorted expression on his face. Five blows. Five hits. What can lie beyond that? Martin will never be able to see beyond this horror.

They drift along.

When he peers over the edge of the boat, the current is carrying him past trees in which children crouch like squirrels and conspiratorially place their fingers to their lips, for in between the roots, bandits are lying on their stomachs in the river, drinking the blood that seeps from their wounds along with the water.

Now and then, a cow with a bloated belly drifts past Martin's boat and then he clings to a hoof so that the boat is hidden behind it.

The river flows uphill. Valley and hill alternate. In the mornings, the fog hangs low. There is moisture on Martin's cheeks and hair; his clothing is damp. At midday, the sun scorches him.

One day, the river grows shallow and makes a bend, and behind the bend there are four horses in the water. The boat drifts towards them; their riders are on the banks. The keel runs aground. Escape would be futile.

Horsemen. Their black cloaks folded back, their sleeves pushed up. They are gutting fish, slitting their bellies with their signet rings, digging out the intestines with their fingers, washing the hollow bellies in the river. They are surprised when they spot Martin.

One rider stomps over. The boy quickly pushes the rooster under the seating plank.

'Look what we have here,' says the horseman and pulls Martin out of the boat by his collar. 'Strange fish today,' he calls over to the others. They laugh in acquiescence. Not everyone likes joking around. They are all extremely bored.

'Too skinny to fry,' one says. 'Throw him back.'

'But I can't swim,' Martin says immediately.

'Damn, the fish can speak,' the man says and sends Martin crashing to the ground. The others roll their eyes.

Martin gets to his feet with a groan. The riders don't know what to do. The boy seizes the moment.

'I want to be a horseman like you,' he says. He only has this one chance.

The riders look at each other, astonished. They ought to burst out laughing. Ought to. But the horsemen are simple men. There is no room for a lot of feelings at the same time. They're still busy being astonished. The rest will follow.

'What do I need to do to become a horseman?' Martin asks, courage taking shape.

One of them clears his throat. 'Boy, let me see your eyes. Look mean. No, you can forget it. Eyes like a saint,' he says. Because everything in Martin's eyes is good and calm.

Now the horsemen bestir themselves. Show some interest.

'You need to be able to fight,' they say. One draws his sword. The other gives Martin his. The child cannot even lift the blade off the ground. They laugh. Two sticks are quickly procured as sword replacements: 'Now raise your weapon, boy.' But Martin does not lift the stick either, even though they are poking and shoving him a little. He doesn't join in.

'I fight with words,' Martin says.

'Oh, really,' one of them says. 'Well, you don't need a horse or a cloak for that.'

'What else do I need to be able to do?'

Laughter, then silence. They think about their skills. Perhaps they are not as accomplished as they thought. They don't really want to cite drinking and whoring, although there are not many who can keep up with them in this regard. It would be wise to throw the child into the river now and to hold it under water for a while. Who is likely to care about a scruffy little boy?

It seems strange to Martin now that the horsemen are so slow to think and act.

Shouldn't a horseman who steals children be sinister, silent and fast? Certainly he would need to be clever. But that does not apply to these men. Are they possibly just a cover for the one, the real horseman?

'What now?' one of them asks.

'He must grow tall,' says another. 'As tall as us. We are alike.'

'I am not like you.'

'Of course you are. I am like you, and you are like me.'

'But I was here first.'

'You are dreaming, dog.'

An argument quickly breaks out. Yes, Martin is certain now that these men have nothing to do with the abduction of the children. They could be from his village. It is such a drag, to keep encountering the same idiots over and over. As if the whole world were full of them, no matter where Martin goes. One has already broken another's nose. They wrestle and roll into the bushes. The two others go and fetch the horses.

'Please. I must come with you,' Martin begs, but they shake him off.

'One of us is still there,' the horseman says and climbs onto his horse. 'We lost him. Back there in the forest.'

Martin's ears immediately prick up. 'Why don't you fetch him?' he asks.

'Werewolves,' another says and climbs onto his horse, speaking down from there as the leather saddle creaks. 'They eat you alive. They start with the feet. They gnaw your bones clean up to your thighs. But you survive that.

They save the rest for the next day. Imagine looking down at your own bloody bones all night and knowing that they will eat you whole the next day.'

'And the pain,' another interjects. 'You keep forgetting to mention the pain.'

'Not everyone is a sissy like you.'

'He's lost, boy. He was from the moment the old witch prophesied it.'

'You are scaring the child,' one of them joked.

'I am not scared,' Martin said.

'Then go and save him. You want to be a horseman, then go and fetch him or take his place – we have work to do.'

'But I get his wife,' someone says from the bushes.

'Believe that if you like,' one of the others says.

'Take me with you,' Martin begs.

The horses prance around the child. He snatches at the hems of the long cloaks and tries to reach the saddles. A howl sounds from the forest. The horsemen's laughter gets stuck in their throats. The fear. The shame. They simply abandoned him. Just left when the wolves came and they were searching for the injured man in the undergrowth. As they do now. They drive their boots into the horses' flanks and charge off. May God judge them; today they are running away from the devils.

16

Martin follows the call of the wolf. The forest is unyielding and dense. Musty darkness envelops him instantly. Horrible undergrowth clings to him. Stinging nettles stand as tall as a man. Wood ants push their way up the trees in spirals. The leaves rustle and behind it all lies a silence, deep and frightening, as if the forest were holding its breath until Martin is completely engulfed by it.

The treetops weave their foliage so densely that he cannot see the sky when he tips his head back.

'Why am I afraid?' Martin asks.

'You are getting closer to your destiny,' says the rooster.

'Have I no choice?'

'Not until you die.'

'Is the horseman still alive? Will I find him?'

The rooster says nothing.

As darkness falls, the howling of the wolves grows louder. They sound closer.

Martin adjusts his steps accordingly; he becomes slower and more cautious, until the twigs under his feet no longer crack.

Then lights flicker towards the child from a hollow. Martin ducks down and slides forwards on his knees. He can hear human voices, laughter and coarse language. Bawling and snatches of song. Cautiously, Martin crawls closer and peeks over the edge of the shallow hollow. He sees a campfire casting its glow on a group of people. Women, men. Surrounded by bundles of clothes. Bundles of people. Crates. Barrels. Rubbish. They bustle around, busy and mindless, drunk and laughing, among the loot they have accumulated, dividing it among themselves, pissing on it, all dignity gone. Chunks of meat are roasting over the fire. Fat hisses in the embers. There is a terrible stink in the air.

Martin clenches his fists. He feels sick.

Chained to a tree, a wolf trembles. It is bleeding from its mouth. Again and again it howls, a lament. A call to its pack. The humans laugh. For a moment Martin thinks the call was in vain. But he is wrong, the wolves are hiding, silent, on the other side of the hollow. Waiting. They cannot do anything yet, cannot help yet. There would be enough of them. They could put all those people to rout down there.

Why don't you do something, Martin wants to ask. They raise their grey heads and look at the child for a moment, then turn their heads back down towards their fellow wolf.

Martin follows the direction of their gaze and only now, picking up on the animals' cue, spots the horseman in the grass. He is tied up and badly injured. His black cloak gleams with blood. Half-upright, he is leaning against a tree stump. His head is slumped to the side. One of the men spits schnapps in his face. The horseman flinches. So he is still alive.

Knives are whetted. Meat is divided up. Some is thrown over to the wolf; it doesn't touch it.

Martin is not only frightened now, he is also very angry. Angry that he has to save the horseman. That he has to see the most terrible thing. Why does he have to discover what no one wants to discover? Why does he have to know that humans are worse than all the demons they fear? Martin cries. He wants to turn around and run away.

Then the rooster nestles its head against the boy's cheek.

'One day,' the rooster whispers. 'One day you will have been here. One day you will know how it all ended. One day you might have nightmares because everything will have been terrible. But you will also be able to relate how easy it was. And that only you could have done it.'

'Easy,' Martin whispers and narrows his stinging eyes.

'Easy,' the rooster repeats. 'For everyone says that I am the devil.'

As he comprehends, Martin has the sense that something is blocking out everything around him and all his actions. All he can hear now is his own heartbeat. He only sees and hears what he does because only he can do it. The devils. The fears. Let the disgusting people over there who are dancing and pushing each other into the fire in their drunken stupor have all their damned superstitions blow up in their faces.

He lowers his hands into the damp earth, here in the shadows, and becomes one himself. Darkens his pale face.

Searches for a few fallen branches, pushes them beneath uprooted tree trunks and beneath loose piles of rocks on the edge of the hollow. Places the rooster on his shoulder now.

Then he shrieks. It is shrill and unbearable. The misery of his short life finds a place in this scream. The sound strikes the people below like icy water poured on their limbs. Their hair stands on end, and for a moment everything stops. They stare at the creature with arms and wings, the double screech from two throats. The ground begins to quake. Tree trunks crash down into the hollow. Rocks rain down on the camp. Hitting one or two people. Crushing a foot, smashing a face. The devil swoops in, claws at heads and crows curses.

'Bael! Bael!' the cannibals scream.

The next moment the wolves are there. Seemingly appearing out of nowhere, they launch themselves at the throats of the men and women. Martin doesn't know whether the rooster gave them the command. Those who are still able to run, flee. They are pursued, hunted, perhaps caught. The howling is driven from the hollow and plunges into the forests.

Then they are gone. Only the dead and the injured remain. Shaking, Martin circles the slain, sidesteps still-twitching hands, ignores the rattling breath of the dying.

He finds the horseman, kneels next to him. And the rider looks at the boy. He knows him. He has seen him before. The horseman's teeth are chattering. Is it fear? Martin moves in closer. Beneath all the mud, his kind face.

'Don't be afraid,' Martin says calmly. 'Don't be afraid.'

17

Martin holds the horse's reins tightly. His knuckles are cracked, raw and bloody. The horse is chewing on the bit and jerking its head up and down. Froth drips onto Martin's clammy hand. The horseman hangs in the saddle and groans.

Since the climb up the narrow path, the castle has been growing up out of the rock like a bony structure. The topmost battlements scratch at the clouds. Above them, rugged sky. The wind is sharp, as if it could cut metal, although it is summer. What would the winter be like? Martin hunches his shoulders. The horse is walking by itself. Its hooves know every bend of the path up the slope.

The castle is strange and cold. A rough block with narrow windows. Not particularly well fortified, but no one wants to be up here anyway. This is where all the bad things in the world come from, Martin thinks.

They arrive at the open gate. Martin leads the horse through the archway. The stones are slippery. The horse loses its footing; the horseman groans. Then they are in the

courtyard, and immediately the obligatory misery begins –
the houses, animals and people required to run a castle.

Everything is quite without splendour. Houses have
gathered in the shadows of the castle walls like an infes-
tation. An entire town has grown in the tightest of spaces.

Pigs grunt their way through puddles. Chickens stalk
through the dirt. The first people approach, the curious
ones who have spotted the child and the horseman. Martin
does not need to explain anything and is not asked either.
They know the horseman. They help him off the horse.
Everyone suddenly helps him off the horse and carries him
away so hastily that Martin struggles to keep up. It is his
horseman. He has earned him.

A woman comes running, with children in tow; she
claps her hands over her mouth. Astonished and happy,
horrified and scared. Everything at once. It must be his
wife. His children. They are hanging from her skirts so
that she can barely move forwards. The half-dead, pain-
wracked horseman is out of her reach. Martin picks up
the youngest child and takes it in his arms, quite matter-
of-factly, and follows the group that has formed around
the woman and the injured man. He needs to stay close.
Simply just stay close. The group moves between the
narrow houses. Washing hangs out to dry above their
heads.

But why does a horseman live in such a miserable hovel?
It is barely large enough for everyone to fit in and place him
on the bed. The curious people sweep pots off the stove
and chairs to the ground with their backsides. The little

ones are almost trampled. A cat jumps from neck to neck, hissing venomously.

Once the horseman has been set down on the bed, everyone backs away from him. Now the wife has the opportunity to approach him. She briefly places her hand on his cheek. It seems he has grown thin on his sickbed in the forest. Someone has sent for a doctor. The wife undoes the bandage and removes the leaves and the herb paste that Martin has spread on the wound. She seems surprised at the sight of the wound. Nods appreciatively.

'Which herbs did you use?' she asks the boy. The old knowledge. Martin jiggles the child on his narrow hip.

Then the doctor is there and makes room for himself. He has just eaten and is picking his teeth. First he smells the wound. His nose is red and enlarged; a drop hangs from it. Martin is worried that the drop might end up in the wound, and he knows that the doctor doesn't care how well everything has healed until now, because in a moment he will dig around in the horseman's flesh to look for the healing pus. Another myth, as Martin knows. The infection will break out anew and the horseman will inevitably die. The doctor might as well spew the remains of his lunch into the wound. But what is Martin supposed to say? No one would listen to him. Instead, he thinks of a distraction.

'I found him in the forest,' he says. 'I believe it is a deep sword-thrust in his side.' And he does not specify whether it was the enemy or the other horsemen.

'My name is Martin,' Martin says, and his voice goes up an octave because he sees that the doctor is already rolling up his sleeves, as if that would help in any way, when all the dirt is stuck under his fingernails, in the folds of his skin, just everywhere.

'And I treated the wound.' Panic makes Martin's voice shake. 'I didn't let him die, but it took a long time to get him back on the horse so that I could bring him back here.'

He casts the wife a pleading look. She picks it up, understands and quickly wraps the bandage around the wound. The doctor looks indignant, but she manages to pacify him. Next door, the aunt, she has an amazing boil. Impressive and quite disgusting. Might he be interested? Oh yes, he would much rather take a look at that than a conventional sword wound. Something different. Up in the castle, there is only constipation and the princess's cough.

'Yes, yes,' says the woman and pushes him out. 'A boil as large as a lamb's head.'

She also thanks the neighbours. She waves and nods until they have all left. Then she closes the low door. It is almost dark in here now. The woman takes the child from Martin's hip.

'We thought he wasn't coming back,' she said.

'Is that why they penned us into this stable?' the horseman asks, half sitting up in his bed.

The woman looks at her fingers. They once embroidered damask, held teacups and plucked the strings of a lute. Now all they do is scrub the floor and the pots, peel potatoes, day in, day out, wipe blobs of snot from her children's noses and steal the hens' eggs from their nests. And from now on they must care for the horseman, who will never get well again. Who will never recover from lying in the forest with his life seeping into the moss. Who finds himself unable to forget how the child staged that terror, a haunting without compare in this world.

Martin realises that the horseman cannot be thankful.

The horseman does not want to be a burden to his wife. He loves his children and wants to set them an example and be strong. Not groaning on his bed, with wounds that will torment him for the rest of his life, in a hut to which his family has been cast out, when before they lived in rooms in the castle. Every morning, he had walked over to the proud horses in the stables. A good life. And now...

Martin does not feel pity for the horseman. The price for his good life was the stolen children. How many might he have abducted?

'He won't stay,' the horseman says.

'He is staying,' the woman says, and pulls Martin in close.

'It's worst at night,' Martin whispers.

'That's always the way,' she says.

'I showed him the stars.'

'Thank you for bringing him back to me.'

She knows it won't be easy. But he is there. And that is better than if he weren't.

'You can stay with us. We will make up a bed for you,' she says. 'Next to the stove. You'll be taken care of.'

Martin smiles. And later, when he curls up on his bed, he feels quite comfortable. He falls asleep to the sound of the other children's breathing, and when, in the night, the horseman wakes his wife and half the town with his loud screams, Martin is sleeping peacefully for the first time in many nights and does not wake up. His slumber is so deep, his exhaustion so great.

18

There is a commotion in the early hours of the morning.

'Lucifer!' comes the shouting from the houses. 'The demons! For God's sake, they are coming through the ceiling now!'

Martin immediately jumps up from behind the bedstead, the cauldron, knocks over some logs.

But the actual noise is coming from the roof, from which clattering and bleating can be heard, loud scraping and then a crash, then a hoof suddenly breaks through the roof and gets stuck.

'The accursed is showing himself!' the horseman groans, as pale as death.

'The devils!' people outside shriek.

The wife calms the crying children. She is not afraid. The hoof wriggles above the stove. Martin takes a closer look. It's a goat, nothing more, he thinks.

'Wife!' the horseman shouts.

'Just that damned Thomann,' the wife says.

But Martin storms out of the door. The sky is grey outside. The sound of cursing comes from the row of low houses. And sure enough, Martin sees a couple of goats clattering across the roofs. The body of a billy goat protrudes from their own roof. It's a long, scrawny animal whose hoof has broken through and who is now jerking back and forth, trying to free itself.

A figure jumps out of the damp mist and looks down at the child.

'Allow me to introduce myself,' the man says. 'Thomann.' He drags the goat by the horns from the roof. The broken timbers clatter to the ground inside the house.

'Rotten grazing this morning,' Thomann says apologetically and throws the billy goat from the roof. It hits the ground hard alongside Martin, but quickly recovers and stares at Martin from three cold eyes. Thomann laughs, rounds up the other goats and throws them from the roofs, from which shouts for the Almighty continue to sound. Then he jumps down himself.

He is tall, with loose limbs in two-tone trousers. Martin stares after him as he disappears in the shadows of the castle.

'The jester,' the woman explains later, when Martin asks her about him.

There isn't much damage. Martin covers the hole.

'It will do,' he tells the horseman.

'Until I do it properly,' the horseman says.

'Until you do it,' Martin says.

'Until I can go back up there.'

'Yes.'

19

The rooster is more cheerful than usual this morning and, to Martin's surprise, prefers to go out on its own. The reason, however, quickly becomes clear – there are several hens nearby.

As for Martin, he goes on his rounds. He soon realises that word has got out about him and the horseman. The inhabitants of the castle town waver between suspicion and admiration when they encounter him. He will need allies to survive this.

So he takes the road to the castle gate. The guard, equipped with a lance and a sword, is chewing on an apple. The lance is immediately lowered in his direction. The guard shakes his head.

'Am I not allowed to go in?' Martin asks.

'You could be anyone,' the guard says.

'I saved the horseman.'

'All right then.'

Martin's face brightens, but the man laughs.

'No, boy. I don't care.'

'But perhaps the princess does care. Perhaps you are making a mistake.'

The man flicks the apple core at Martin.

'If I am not allowed in, who is?' Martin asks.

The man sighs, flings his sword up in the air and catches the naked blade with the palms of his hands. 'Witches with sixteen toes,' he says. 'The executioner, Thomann and pigs that can do arithmetic.'

'I have a rooster that can speak. Would that count?'

The guard spits. 'Even if you could fly bum first, I wouldn't let you in.'

'Would anyone even notice?'

'Jesus. You're as stubborn as my missus.'

Martin scrutinises the man. He is quite young and seems bored. He keeps glancing over to the women flouncing across the courtyard. Every now and then he shudders, shifting his weight from one leg to the other. A slight fever. No…

Martin waits. The man begins to bob up and down impatiently.

'Get lost,' he says to Martin.

The boy takes a few steps backwards, but keeps looking at the man. He has a suspicion and just now needs a bit of patience to confirm it. An insanely agonising itch. Often seen in the village and later in the taverns. And indeed, now the man loses his composure, grabs his crotch and scratches compulsively.

'Pubic lice,' the painter once explained to him. 'If you look who's scratching, you know who's been rolling in the hay with whom.'

Martin is pleased. That's a start at least.

'Get lost,' the guard grumbles.

Happy now, Martin concedes to being sent away.

Over the next few hours, Martin can be observed at the stables, at the walls and elsewhere, gathering grit and chalk, scraping lichen from a wall, asking for a small bowl and patiently grinding the ingredients to a very fine powder.

In the afternoon, he reappears at the gate.

'You again,' the guard growls.

Martin holds the bowl to him. 'Apply it twice a day,' the boy says.

'Apply?'

'To the affected area.'

'What are you talking about?'

'To the areas that itch.'

'What do you care about my itches?'

'I saw that the blond woman in the house over there, the house that you have a perfect view of from your post, also has an itch.'

'Oh.'

'Yes. Her husband doesn't have the same problem. That is strange,' Martin says. 'So if I were you, I wouldn't stand here all day scratching myself in front of everyone. Someone might come up with the bright idea of asking the woman.'

The guard listens to Martin's words. He reaches out his hands for the bowl, very slowly. Martin pulls his hand back just a little.

'What?' the man hisses. He thinks. 'In exchange, I'll let you in.'

'Not right now. I want to go in when it suits me.'

Martin hands him the powder, which the man, turning his back, applies so quickly that white clouds rise up. The guard sighs with relief. And Martin is satisfied. Soon he will go in, but only once he has understood.

20

In the mornings, the sky clings to the castle battlements.

The children like to stick to Martin's heels. He enjoys pretending not to notice the small flock of ducks behind him for a while, then turning around all of a sudden and giving them a fright so that they jump and run, shrieking.

His keen powers of observation make it easy for him to make himself useful everywhere. He can always spot where a helping hand is needed. This makes everyone who likes to stand around idly feel superfluous. It's a bit as if the people up here haven't been able to cope well without Martin. Or they haven't noticed how poorly they have been communicating with one another. As if all those who have lived up here on the princess's hill since they were born have lost the ability to think carefully before they act.

But no matter how many times Martin asks about the missing children, he can't get an answer.

He often watches Thomann. The jester works with three misshapen goats and three human companions. He tries to teach one group something, then the other. It is not clear which group is quicker on the uptake.

Thomann has cold bright eyes like his goats. He doesn't care what people say. Sometimes he is loud and friendly, juggling with apples that he gives away to the children. He juggles with eggs that he lets burst – when he intends them to. Sometimes he mimics people, and no one is safe from the silent ridicule with which he follows them, imitating their posture and facial expression – it's exquisite, as if two versions of the same person were walking along.

Today, he has erected a frame of narrow boards, ladders and rings, on which he balances while the goats stand and stare.

'What are you doing?' Martin asks.

'What am I doing?' Thomann asks back. He knows the boy – a diversion amid the dull castle dwellers.

'You are climbing,' Martin says.

Thomann has reached a point where he can only put one foot in front of the other. The beam bends. The entire scaffolding seems shaky and temporary. He could have learned a lot from the painter, Martin thinks.

'But why are you doing it?' the boy asks.

'I want to understand the goats,' the man says and falls off the beam, gets back on his feet and dusts down his trousers. 'You know, goats think all day long. Shall I tell you what they think? They think: baa, baa and baa and sometimes baabaa. Yes,' he sighs, 'they are wonderful animals.' Then he rustles a small sack that dangles from his hip. 'They also love eating carrots.'

The first goat immediately jumps effortlessly onto the frame. The second follows suit; only the third refuses.

'That's because of her third eye,' Thomann says and gives the animal a comforting pat. 'She can't see straight, but she can see into the future.'

'Really?' Martin asks and earns a surprised look.

'You didn't know?' Thomann takes the goat's head between his hands and speaks into the animal's nostrils. 'Tell me, Master, the future of this boy.'

Then he listens, as does Martin.

'Do you hear its reply?' the jester whispers.

'I can hear it,' Martin whispers back.

'And? What is it saying?' Thomann asks.

'Baa,' Martin says. 'It says baa, baa and sometimes baa-baa.'

Thomann bursts into laughter and exaggerates a bit as he does so. That's because he probably hasn't heard a clever thought or a surprising joke for five years. And he is less and less convinced by his own ideas too. Martin is a bit offended. Do adults have to take children for idiots? When Martin has already looked into every abyss? Or maybe not yet. If there is still one for which he will have to give his all, then he will find it here at the castle. He knows it.

Thomann offers him a carrot. They chew together as they watch the goats climbing.

'What do you do here?' Martin finally asks once more.

'I entertain the princess,' the jester says. 'From time to time she wants to have fun, and then I come and make her laugh, cry and marvel, and then I am allowed to sleep in a golden bed with my goats and drink honey.'

Thomann throws half a carrot to his animals.

'A golden bed?' Martin repeats.

'Yes, damn it. Look at me. Don't I deserve it?' Thomann says and tugs at his trousers, which are stiff with dirt. 'Jesters are respected everywhere, they are the real kings alongside the queen. Except here. Just not here on this goddamned hill.'

'So why don't you go somewhere else?' Martin asks.

'You can't just leave.'

'I left,' Martin said.

Thomann shakes his head. 'I will never go. I won't leave this castle until I can fly,' he says. And after a while, he adds: 'Come, I'll show you the best spot and the reason why I can't leave.'

21

Martin quickly learns that a jester has ways and obligations just like a farmer, waggoner and miller. The sidekicks need to be paid. They need to be admonished, slapped and told when to reconvene. Martin follows him on his rounds. Thomann needs food. He goes to see Hansel. Takes a deep long sniff of a piece of meat.

'That's so old it can walk of its own accord,' he grumbles and goes on to dump a scoop of flour, teeming with maggots, at Hansel's feet. 'I want to bake bread, not catch fish.'

Thomann is diligent. He has work to do. In between two errands, he cracks dirty jokes that cause the merchant to grin and show his damaged set of teeth, and the women to blush. He conjures chickens from children's ears and sausages from their noses. But then he heads back to his home. It seems to be important to him, although he is really only ever seen with his goats. Pottering around and practising in a shelter, he never seems to be anything else but a jester in two-tone trousers. And now he has a home at the end of the road, on the perimeter of the castle. A home and someone waiting for him.

A girl opens the door, perhaps a young woman, Martin can't really say, she has the face of a scallywag; it is ageless. Her nose is very small, her mouth on the other hand extremely large. Her eyes are black, her ears stick out. Tangled hair around her head. A tiny person. She gives the jester a long hug. Then she hugs Martin.

'There you two are, at last,' she says as if she already knows about Martin, as if she hasn't seen the jester for a long time.

'This is Marie,' he introduces her. 'My sister.'

'What a beautiful creature you have there,' Marie says. 'What is it?'

'A rooster.'

'A rooster. How wonderful. Very unusual. Do come in,' she says.

Martin follows her into the dark room. It is cold. There is no fire in the hearth. Bugs are dripping from the walls.

'Do take a seat,' Marie says and offers a chair. But the chair is piled high with all sorts of things. There are things lying around everywhere that don't seem to make sense. Thomann doesn't comment on it. Whenever he goes past Marie, she flings her arms around him.

'I like you so much,' she sighs.

'I like you too,' he says patiently. Every time. He throws Martin a blanket. 'Marie is scared of fire.'

'How was your journey?' Marie asks, and smiles at Martin with her wide mouth from a world that he doesn't know.

A world in which there is only friendliness. Marie chatters. 'How is the weather where you come from?' she asks.

'Cold,' Martin says.

'Oh yes. Cold is not nice,' Marie interjects. 'You are lucky that you have a pet.'

'And you have him.'

'Yes, I am so happy. But sometimes he is gone, and I must wait. Then I am frightened. Oh, how I am frightened! It is not nice.'

Marie's eyes fill with tears. Thomann comes back over and puts some food on the table. A meal for Marie and one for Martin.

'Thank you, I am very hungry,' Marie says and looks at the food. 'What are we having?'

'Milk and soaked bread.'

'Oh, thank you, too kind. I like milk and soaked bread.' And she never eats anything else, but Martin doesn't know that yet.

Martin gets sausage and cheese, with an onion on the side. Thomann drinks wine. It is very cold. Marie takes only tiny bites of her food. But she talks.

'Did everything go well on the journey?' she asks. And: 'Did you meet anyone you know?' She asks: 'How was the weather?' She asks: 'What was the name of the place where you come from?'

Martin tells her the name and thinks nothing of it.

But Marie looks inside herself, into her small, tidy soul, where the few experiences of her life are lined up nicely next to the friendliness, as if they were waiting to be looked at again and again, so that one could chat about them. 'I've heard of that place. We have had a visitor from there before.'

'Really?' says Martin and suddenly can't chew his food. His hands feel like they are stuck to the table. He feels as if the whole room is turning upside down until the wine flows out of the jester's glass and the milk drips out of Marie's hair.

'A very nice man. I remember him well. He had eyes just like yours.'

'Eyes like mine?' Martin says.

And the walls dissolve. And the floor slides away.

'Such a nice man. He wanted to pass the princess's sleeping test. To save his village. They were in debt. You understand? Hardly anything left to eat on the fields. They drove the cattle into the forests so that they could find something to eat.'

'Lichen and moss. Bark and mushrooms,' Martin says quietly. He knows the story.

'And they had a Lisl in the village, who had seizures and said that the game had to be won once, so that the taxes wouldn't be so high. And then she never—'

'—said anything clever again,' Martin continues her sentence. Sentences that hold his childhood memories. Delicate and unnoticed. Never important and now suddenly in Marie's mouth. Why?

'And then he came to play the game.'

'A poor fool like all the others who try it,' Thomann says, while Martin's world disappears behind Marie. Behind

Marie's wide mouth, which talks and – can it be? – speaks of his father.

'Unfortunately, he didn't win, did he?' says Marie, and hovers above Martin like a goddess.

'No one can win the sleep game,' Thomann says.

What happened to him, Martin thinks.

'It was probably too much for him,' Marie replies. 'He behaved quite strangely afterwards. He was very scared. They say that he ran all the way home. It must have been very tiring.'

'He went mad,' the jester says.

Martin falls off his chair and bangs his head.

'I am tired too,' says Marie and lies down next to him. Thomann spreads a blanket over them both.

Marie hugs Martin like his sister probably would have done. She is so innocent that she falls asleep faster than anyone else. She smiles in her sleep. She does not loosen her hold on Martin.

The jester puts on a black cloak, pulls a hood over his head and reaches for the axe. 'You can stay,' he says.

'Who are you now?' Martin asks weakly.

'I am the executioner. My father was an executioner too. I have work to do,' Thomann says. The executioner says.

'Then you are both?' Martin says and closes his eyes.

'Yes, I have plenty to do,' says the jester. Says the executioner.

And Martin thinks, yes, that makes sense, because it doesn't make sense and it is all wrong, just like the rest of this damned world.

22

Bit by bit, rules for life in the castle reveal themselves. That is to say, rules are arbitrarily added or tightened, but never abandoned. There is a nebulous basic principle, the rest is luck or misfortune, and it is best to proceed with fear and mistrust. Nonetheless, there are of course transgressions. Martin will find out today how the punishment for those works. And all without the intervention of the executioner, for although the post is occupied, unfortunates are killed everywhere in other and more terrible ways than by the axe. Perhaps the axe is not exciting enough for the princess?

A tree called the Ladies' Tree grows in the castle courtyard. Martin has often asked why it is called that, but has never received an answer. Just as there are no straightforward answers to most questions here, but rather some things just explain themselves at some point.

The tree is withered and tall, with wide branches; no one knows exactly what kind of tree it is. The branches are gnarled like those of a fruit tree, but the trunk is long and slender. In spring, the people wait eagerly to see which leaves will appear. So far they have been different each year. This year it had none at all and was bare long before it should have been, but on this day, which brings the first autumnal downpour, it bears a pretty female corpse.

She is suspended by her hair, which has twined itself around numerous branches and become entangled. When the wind blows, her skirts billow back and forth, and her body sways gently. Her face is pale and beautiful; a young lady of the court in a pale blue dress. The delicate shoes have slipped off her feet. Some children have snatched them up and are stumbling around in them. A crowd stands sadly beneath the dead woman.

'It is not nice when the Ladies' Tree bears fruit. Even if what it bears is beautiful,' Thomann says.

'What happened to her?' Martin asks.

The horseman's wife places her arms around his shoulders. 'Don't talk to him,' she says.

'I will talk to him,' Martin says, and then to Thomann: 'So, what did she do?' – because he does not care about the possessiveness that is stirring in the two adults. Both like the child and want him for themselves, but Martin belongs only to his task of finding the abducted children. And he doesn't forget that, regardless of how motherly the woman's hand on his shoulder has grown in the meantime. Regardless of how fascinated he is by Thomann. At night, the boy still shares his bed with the rooster, and nothing can make him forget Godel's hand hanging empty in the air when the horseman took the little girl.

'One of the princess's ladies-in-waiting,' Thomann says quietly. 'Probably too pretty and therefore a thorn in her side.'

The woman clenches her lips and says nothing. She places her hand on her stomach, which is now clearly swelling. She is expecting another child and often feels nauseous.

'The princess can get very grumpy when someone is younger and more beautiful.' And, in the nature of things, this is becoming more and more of an issue for the princess. 'That is why the Ladies' Tree sometimes bears a beautiful corpse. What a waste,' he sighs.

Two men appear with a ladder. One of them holds a long knife.

'Now she will be harvested,' Thomann says. The horseman's wife starts crying.

'What is the knife for?' Martin asks.

And then he quickly understands. The hair, seemingly inextricably entwined, is to be cut off so that they can remove the corpse from the tree. It will be a final humiliation for the dead woman. Probably quite to the princess's liking.

But Martin doesn't allow it. He already has a rope in his hand and has climbed up the ladder. He instructs the men, while the people below watch. The rope is put around the dead woman's waist, then the end of the rope is thrown over a branch and pulled. Now the body is dangling from the rope, no longer by its hair. Martin sends the men away and starts to climb the tree, light and agile like a bird, untangling strand after strand from the branches. Even when it starts to rain harder, he pulls the hair from the branches hour after hour, making sure the dead woman can keep her curls. Most probably he cries a little, and of course the people only watch him in amazement for the first few hours. And they most certainly feel ashamed, because thus far they have never had the courage to give the dead ladies-in-waiting some of their dignity back.

What is certain is that the princess watches from her window for a while as the boy clambers around in the Ladies' Tree. What a fuss! But she doesn't care.

She already knows that autumn is coming. Soon the cranes will come and there are more important things to do. And for the moment she feels quite good, now that she has tidied up a bit among the ladies-in-waiting, which should be a lesson to the others. Who was to know that what had been a bony and spotty ward of fourteen would one day turn into such a beauty? She will be more careful in the future about who she takes under her wing. Or not. Because the Ladies' Tree is actually a cherished tradition.

23

A restlessness spreads among the inhabitants of the castle town. It saturates their thoughts and deeds. Everyone seems to be feverish, looking up at the sky constantly.

'What are the people waiting for?' Martin asks the rooster.

'Autumn is coming,' the rooster says.

'I have never seen people waiting for autumn like this before,' says Martin. 'Why don't they collect provisions?'

But before the rooster on his shoulder can reply, Thomann appears next to him. He has crept up silently like a snake. Has he heard the rooster?

'There is no point preparing,' he says. 'No stewed apples or flour fit only for mice are going to help with what's coming.'

'What is coming?'

'Oh, son,' Thomann says. 'You should leave. But if you don't, spare me any complaints that I didn't warn you.'

'Warn me about what?' Martin asks.

The jester shakes his head and refuses to answer.

But he does ask: 'How do you make the rooster speak? The art of ventriloquism? Why didn't you tell me that you have mastered it?'

Martin doesn't know what he is talking about.

'You should perform with us. Tomorrow, before the princess. It's her last celebration of the year. Would you like to?'

A thought flashes through Martin's mind. Enter the castle. See the princess. Of course he wants to. Thomann takes him by the hand.

'We'll go through it all,' he says and takes Martin with him to the shelter. He doesn't stop until they reach the goats and his companions. The goats are chewing on carrots, his companions on onions. They have the same witless expressions. One of them is crying and wipes his eyes for a long time. Is it because of the onion? Only when he lowers his hands does Martin recognise him. He suspected it a few times, from afar, and now he is sure. It is the horrible child.

It is the child that once swung himself on Martin's back and drove him through the mud. In the meantime, the child has grown up; he is almost a man. Big-boned, soft in the hips, shaggy hair. And the voice. The luminous voice that came from his throat, where is it now? Martin is overcome by the strange feeling that he is no longer travelling forwards but backwards. As if everything would be turning back from now on, or returning. Martin stares at the nasty boy.

'Stop crying. Show what you've learned today,' Thomann admonishes him.

The detestable brat sniffs, then drools a bit until there's foam around his mouth, tosses his head back and forth, squints and pretends to be a madman.

'Who wants to see that?' Thomann sighs. 'Can't you perhaps recite a few French rhymes?'

'I can only do the thing with the spit,' the boy whinges. 'No one told me I had to speak French.'

'All right, all right,' the jester appeases. 'What else can you do?'

'He can sing like an angel,' Martin says.

'You know him?'

'His voice was pure light.'

'Yes, yes. And now he can fart on demand.'

'I can indeed,' the boy shouts, and demonstrates his skill.

'God almighty,' Thomann says.

'I can even do a song!'

'The Lord God is immeasurable in his mercy, but also incomprehensible.'

'And what can he do?' one of them asks, pointing at Martin.

'He is entertaining,' the jester says. 'Give him something to wear.'

When Martin appears a little later in colourful tights and an embroidered doublet, it doesn't meet with approval.

'You look like my son,' Thomann groans.

At dinner with the horseman's family, Martin doesn't tell them that he will be heading to the castle with Thomann the next morning. He is friendly as always. He fetches wood and helps the horseman to lift his legs, which have become thin, over the edge of the bed, supports him until he can sit up by himself.

Martin struggles to fall asleep that night. The restlessness is in him too now. He thinks he can hear the entire town twisting and turning in circles, like one of those clockwork carousels. It can make you dizzy.

It is daybreak by the time Martin falls asleep.

24

'If the princess likes our performance,' Thomann says, 'we'll be pelted with cake.'

'Cake?' Martin asks.

'Don't tell me you've never eaten any?'

The jester, Martin, the companions and the three goats head towards the castle gate. The guard with the powder waves the performers through, then hastily does the same for Martin.

Martin's heart almost stops when they enter. He is finally getting closer to the mystery. His footsteps, in his wooden clogs, clatter across the stone floor together with the goats' hooves. It is cold inside the castle walls. Colder than outside. Everything grabs Martin's attention. Vases, furniture, servants. Chambermaids tugging at their skirts as if they had visitors beneath them. Rats scurrying into the corners. Wounded men with bulging scars on their faces and missing limbs. He sees horsemen. They are also invited to the celebration. They have taken off their cloaks, but Martin has not forgotten their faces from the river.

Colourful birds flutter under the ceilings. Their plumage is yellow and light green; they have little rose-red heads and crooked beaks. They perch on candlesticks and armchairs. They bill and coo, and pluck out feathers. Soft fluff sails through the air like snowflakes. There are bird droppings everywhere. The floor is speckled all over. The paintings on the walls grow ever more similar, as large as doors, framed in gold, curdling into a motif which is always the same: a woman with a new-born in her arms. To the left and right, two serious, beautifully dressed children. A boy of about eight, and a girl, probably ten. A long blond plait, and so like Godel's daughter – as if they were sisters, as if it were her. On all these paintings. How can that be?

'Who is that woman?' Martin quietly asks the jester, who is striding jauntily through the corridors.

'That is the princess,' Thomann whispers back, and scoffs: 'Our eternal new mother.'

And Martin feels very cold. Painting after painting. Corridor after corridor. The children stare down at Martin from all the paintings.

The hall. They reach it with all the others. The ladies of the court and the horsemen. The servants with fruit platters and towers of meat. The songbirds that fly in and out. And so they all clatter and jostle into the hall full of lit candles and a horribly exuberant atmosphere that speaks of too much wine and the fear of being dead tomorrow. A long table stands in the middle of the hall.

Someone claps their hands. The giggles die down; the erratic gestures search for a fold of clothing to rest on.

Then the curtain on the other side of the room parts and a wide bed slides in as if by magic. What a nightmare, Martin thinks.

On the bed, the princess. Old and horribly made-up. Too much red on her lips, her slack skin chalky white, circular spots on her cheeks. She, who could easily be a grandmother, carries a bundle in her arms. A tiny infant. Children sit alongside her, dressed and trained. Their huge pupils are dilated by deadly nightshade juice. It makes them submissive and obedient. Too much of it kills. The girl looks so much like Godel's daughter. But it is not her. Why is her double sitting here?

The princess nods benevolently to all sides. It is all just a facade. Martin recognises the hideous face behind it. What is she doing to the children? What has she been doing with the children all these years? Always the same age. The same face. But always new. Always fresh.

Martin realises that she swaps them. She swaps them as soon as they grow older and change, perhaps no longer corresponding to the strict guidelines. Perhaps displeasing her. She swaps them for new children. And these then again for new children. How long has Martin known the story of the horseman who steals children? How long has she been doing this?

Martin blacks out. He slumps down, but Thomann catches him. There's a murmur, a bit of curiosity. The jester loses his smile; he has been counting on the boy. The rooster rises up from beneath Martin's shirt. The princess beckons Thomann over.

'What is the matter with the boy?' she asks as leniently as she wishes she could be day in, day out. Mild and likeable. If only there wasn't so much to do and she wasn't surrounded by stupid subjects.

'Who is this? I don't know him.'

Thomann is holding the unconscious boy. He is so light. The man is searching for a suitable reply that might please the princess, when the rooster replies for him: 'This is the child that saved the horseman.'

The princess gawps at the animal. Then she shrieks. In fright. In delight. There is too much colour in her face for the true emotion to be clearly readable. Who is playing the fool here, the jester thinks.

'What a wonderful thing!' the princess calls out. 'Can it do anything else?'

'You are not listening,' says the rooster. 'The child saved the horseman. He is a hero.'

The princess laughs shrilly. 'Magnificent! Fabulous!' and praises Thomann. 'How entertaining!'

'Yes,' he says, not really knowing what is happening. Who is talking? The child's eyes are rolled back. His breath is shallow. How can he be throwing his voice? The rooster flaps its wings. The princess coughs. The new-born sways in front of her chest. The children on the bedcovers stare into space with their flickering eyes.

'What beautiful children you have,' the rooster says.

'A flatterer!' the old woman laughs.

Thomann grins wryly and makes a graceful bow. What else can he do? Then Martin comes round. Some might think that the faint was a sign of weakness, but it is not so. Martin comes round with clear thoughts and a strengthened heart. He is entirely focused again, on a truth that lies beyond all prudence. And so he bows awkwardly and says: 'Children show us how time passes.'

The impudence of it. The inconceivability of addressing the evil that the princess has spun around herself.

'Are you mad?' Thomann hisses, while Martin still struggles to hold his head straight. But it is no struggle to take the path that has been laid out for him. Step by step, until it is done.

The princess's face, which has just been amused, collapses. The white colour bursts in chunks from her cheeks. 'Enough chitchat,' she says.

Thomann takes Martin aside. The man knows the princess. She does not act on impulse. She enjoys thinking up her punishments. She can be very creative when it comes to avenging a disgrace in such a way that it will be obliterated forever. Perhaps the rest of the performance can mitigate the sentence. Hastily he beckons his companions to start their antics.

They begin juggling over the furniture, with everything they can get their hands on. Thomann also lets the goats loose. They hop onto the laid table without trampling on a single plate or knocking over a single glass, although one of them does leave some droppings among the dark grapes. But for a magical moment, all three of them manage to stand one on top of the other. The goat with the three eyes is on the top. The crowning glory of all creatures. Its triumphant bleating pierces everyone's marrow and bone.

But the moment has already passed, and the goats have forgotten that they are drilled and graceful. Instead, they start kicking. Two ladies-in-waiting pay the price with their incisors. A chandelier starts to sway. Crystal shatters. The entire party starts moving. Here is the splattered blood of the ladies-in-waiting, there the burning tablecloth, the goats hopping around everywhere, the jugglers trying to catch them. Everything breakable is broken.

At first Thomann tries to intervene, but then he realises that the hour is irrevocably lost. Perhaps also his life. But isn't that irrelevant, when the chaos is so delightfully comical?

The three-eyed goat manages to jump onto the princess's bed. You have to love it for that. Until now, the princess has also been enjoying the tumult. For what do dishes or ladies-in-waiting's teeth matter, what does it all matter in comparison to the delight of a good joke, or the laughter that is so rare in all the dreary hours of being a ruler? In the boredom which can only be relieved by cruelty? For cruelty is easy. But a good joke is hard to find. The princess even finds the billy goat on her bed amusing, but then the animal lifts the new-born from her arms with firm lips and jumps away with it.

Thomann roars with laughter. Truly.

Martin is astonished at how agile the billy goat is as it hops around with the doll, because yes, it is a doll and everyone has seen it. Won't they all have to have their eyes gouged out now? Of course everyone knows that the princess does not give birth to a new-born year after year and carry it with her. But knowing and seeing are not the same thing. And it is taboo to see what is known, to speak of it, to think of it or to dream of it. That means death.

Someone will have to pay. No one dares to stop the goat. No one dares to take the doll, the tyrant's precious treasure.

Then the princess utters a scream. And the jester decides to sacrifice himself, for he will not live to see a better joke than this. So he might as well die.

He grabs the goat and wraps the doll in a blanket. He steps towards the princess. The colour on his face has run with tears of laughter. There are similar traces on the princess's face. How similar they are now, like swashbucklers in a story. Like the last of a fading epoch.

And now the end.

He carefully places the doll in her arms.

'You are going before the executioner,' she says with a quivering voice.

'Hmm,' Thomann says. 'That is going to be difficult.'

The princess realises that she hasn't thought it through. The jester is the executioner. Who decided on this nonsense?

'There is no going back,' she says.

'But there is no going forwards either. What with suicide being a mortal sin.'

They are not exactly well versed in the Bible in the castle, but they know about mortal sins.

'I will ask my councillors,' she says.

'Your councillors are as thick as two short planks. Shall my jester's soul wander through hell for eternity? We can ask the child. He is clever,' he says, and points to Martin.

But before the coughing princess can even think of remembering the boy and perhaps also sentence him to death for his remarks, they hear the unmistakable calls in the sky.

Martin knows the sound. Autumn echoes through the world. The princess's eyes turn milky.

'The cranes,' she says tonelessly. 'The cranes are coming.'

25

Two bird migrations have to cross the mountains to find their way south. They fly low, almost touching the castle battlements. Feathers rain down. The formations overlap, drift towards one another, away from one another. Their calls evoke a sadness, as if they were heralding a more beautiful world that will always be out of reach for the castle's inhabitants. And that is how it is. How many of them there are! You could almost touch them.

Martin watches. The others have also stepped out of their houses. Some of them hug each other, trying to give comfort. The horseman's wife strokes her belly.

'Where were you?' she asks Martin.

Martin can't find the words. She pulls him away. Away from Thomann, who marches to his shelter, whistling as if he's had a good day and not just been given his death sentence. He does not turn around for Martin.

The horseman is sitting up on the edge of the bed in the house, supporting himself with his arms. He has a stick nearby. Is he practising getting up? And why today of all days? Sweat is running down the horseman's temples, yet it is freezing cold in here. Martin checks the fire and starts to feed it.

'Use the wood sparingly,' the wife says. 'You may only use, drink or eat half of everything you usually do from now on.'

'What happens now?'

'The horsemen leave,' she says.

'They close the gate,' her husband says. 'No more goods. No more traders. No more hunted game, no fish from the river, no ducks. Nothing from outside until the men return.'

'Why?' Martin asks.

The horseman remains silent, staring into the faint glow.

'A curse,' the wife says wearily. 'It seems it has always been the way. The flight of the cranes, followed by the dark time. We must atone. Only if we atone and stick together can we resist the demons. Then the horsemen return and everything starts over again. Better, maybe. That's what the princess says.'

The princess is mad, Martin thinks. And mad people invent mad rules.

'It's your last chance to leave,' the horseman says urgently. 'They won't let you out later.'

'I don't want to leave,' Martin says. Not yet. Not before it is over.

'One more mouth to feed,' the horseman says.

'He doesn't need much,' says the wife.

'I can help,' says Martin.

'You already do help,' says the wife.

Martin thinks of the children who are living out their lives, who are with their parents and thinking they are safe. Until the horsemen find them and their fate has to be linked to that of the castle's inhabitants.

How awful, Martin thinks, how unbearable.

The horsemen gather in the courtyard. Hooves scrape across the stones by the gate. It is impossible to guess what the horseman who is staying behind is thinking. His gaze is turned inwards. Is he searching his heart for the children that he found and took? How many did he abduct? How many are on his conscience?

'Half of everything,' Martin says quietly, counting out the potatoes, while the big gate is closed outside. Its hinges screech as if they were announcing doom.

26

You can't describe it. You want to close your eyes. You would rather be blind and deaf, so that you don't have to watch the slow decline. Even the slightest blink of the eye sends an image into your soul and poisons it. At night, demons and ghosts hunt across the castle courtyard. There is howling outside the doors; no one can sleep. Martin knows that the princess is sending these devils. She sends them so that no one dares to question her decision.

The fear of fire is great. There is nowhere to go. During the day, a thick fog envelops the castle. There is no other world except the one between the huts. And all order has disappeared. Folk suffocate in their filth.

Councillors come from the castle and read proclamations. Everyone is tasked to stand together against the curse. Soup is distributed. But there are barely any vegetables in the broth. No meat, of course. In the apples that are given out, the autumn rot has decomposed the flesh. And the bread that the princess has thrown out of the windows is so hard it could kill enemies.

'Which is why we are considered impregnable,' quips Thomann, who bumbles around incessantly in his draughty shelter and soon has a bad cough that makes him sound like a hound from hell.

'I need to work faster,' he says to Martin. 'If I don't hurry up, the cough will probably kill me before I can be my own executioner.'

'Isn't that actually the same thing?' Martin says.

'You could have been a philosopher, you know,' Thomann says and carries on working without revealing what it is he's building. And no one cares except Martin anyway. The others forget him because he no longer roams around making his jokes. Or because everyone is busy trying to manage their own affairs. Is it worth getting out of bed in the mornings? Is there any point being nice to the neighbour when it is not clear who will survive the dark times?

Martin walks hand in hand with hunger again as if it were a familiar friend. The horseman also laughs at the hunger and says that at least then his body won't be so heavy. He practises every day and raises himself up with his stick. He doesn't want to go anywhere, and couldn't anyway; he just wants to seem as if he has recovered and is strong. He is protective above all.

For you have to be protective. And alert. The hopelessness of the place, the fear-ridden time, quickly makes many mean. Often someone bangs against the door to test what the response is. Some even dare to ask for hidden supplies or doubt whether the horseman can protect his wife and children. If someone is too weak, everything that is not nailed down is snatched away. Simply because it doesn't matter.

'Only those with few standards survive times like these, because goodness and honour need enough to eat,' the horseman says.

'There are exceptions,' says Martin.

'There are exceptions,' the horseman repeats.

And when every so often a curious face appears at the window, when whisperers slink around the house and scratch at the thin walls, the horseman finally drags himself over to the door.

'Stand behind me and prop me up,' he says to Martin.

The boy does so, pushing his back against the big man, who puts the stick aside and pushes the door open.

The troublemakers – the horseman knows them all – jump back a few metres and get a proper fright. But they scurry back again right away. The horseman holds himself straight. His arms loosely crossed, his legs firmly planted in the ground, as if it were completely normal.

'Well, little rider,' one of the cheeky ones says. 'Haven't seen you so perky for a long time.'

'What do you want?' the horseman asks.

'Just to see how you are doing. You got us thinking.'

'Not usually your forte. Thinking as such.'

The other man grinned. 'I am just saying. You are usually out and about. Up on your horse and all that. We used to wait for you, boy oh boy. And now you have to wait and you are stuck here. Not everyone can deal with that.'

'Yes,' the horseman says. 'Anything else?'

'Huh?' the other man says.

'No?' the horseman asks. 'I'll tell you something. If I see you and your kind near my family again, you'll never need to wait for anything ever again. Then it will all be behind you.'

The grin on the man's face freezes. Somehow he had pictured the afternoon differently.

The horseman slowly closes the door, which is just as well, because Martin can't hold him for a second longer. And the horseman can't hold himself up either. They manage to make it to the bed, and there they laugh a little over the stupid faces.

That night Martin awakes with a start. The wife is groaning and padding around the room.

'The baby is coming,' she says to Martin. He claps his hands to his mouth in delight. 'How wonderful,' he says.

This boy, the wife thinks gratefully and sobs. This pure child. Yes, it *is* wonderful, if only it weren't happening here at the castle, at night and during the dark times.

'What should I do?' Martin asks.

'You must fetch the midwife,' the horseman says.

'He can't go out. It's not allowed,' the wife says.

'You need the midwife,' the horseman insists.

'This is not my first child,' the wife says.

'Then it is I who need the midwife,' he says.

'But the spirits,' the wife groans, holding her low belly.

'I don't mind,' Martin says. 'Truly. I'll go.' And he is already at the door. He doesn't need a light and there wouldn't have been one for him anyway. The courtyard outside lies in dull grey night that doesn't grow black because the clouds hide the stars. They have been hiding them for weeks. Snow and ice hang in them.

The midwife lives on the other side of the courtyard. Her house nestles close to that of the jester, the executioner. The things that belong together, Martin thinks, and ducks in between the huts. He hears the ghosts howl, but he doesn't believe in them. He thinks that they are only pretend, perhaps puppets, to scare the inhabitants and keep them in check. Or perhaps just because the princess enjoys being gruesome.

And then he is suddenly startled when the narrow door next to the castle gate opens, although no one is allowed out and no one is allowed in until the horsemen return. What does he see? A princely hunter darts across the courtyard towards the castle. Two pheasants, ducks and a rabbit that he has killed are slung over his shoulder. He slips casually across the courtyard. He is not afraid of being caught, even though the ghosts are howling loudly enough to make your hair stand on end. No one dares to look, and so no one notices what Martin now knows and has long suspected. That the princess is not suffering want like everyone else. She is well provided for.

The boy is gripped by anger. He quickly arrives at the midwife's house and knocks, but a scream comes from inside and it takes a long time until the midwife understands what Martin wants, and it takes even longer for Martin to accept her reply. She is not coming. She is too scared and prefers to hide under her bed.

'But you must come!' cries Martin. The midwife puts her hands over her ears and sings a prayer, over and over – just the one. Fear has made her forget the others. And if she just squeezes her eyes tightly enough, the boy will probably disappear too.

'She's not coming,' Martin says when he is back with the horseman and his wife. And so they have to manage by themselves. Martin is full of courage, with a trust in a world that only he has. That he breathes into the child, who struggles to take its first breath.

And when they have managed it and Martin is allowed to hold the tiny creature in his arms, they name it after him.

27

This must be the end. What else can there be? How could dignity ever be restored? And even if it were, the next autumn, the next crane migration would bring about misery once again.

The wife lies with the children in the arms of the horseman, who is embracing them all. He has weathered the hardships. Grey and old, he keeps an eye on the door. But no one has troubled them for a long time. No one has the energy to misbehave.

'It has never gone on for so long before,' says the wife, who tirelessly breastfeeds the baby and the other children to soothe their hungry cries.

Of course it has never gone on for so long, Martin wants to say. Until now, the clever horseman was with the other men. The man who is now protecting his family with the last ounce of his strength and who is wrestling with his conscience. What monstrous thoughts haunt him during his sleepless nights?

Even the rooster has grown thin and seldom speaks any more. But at night, when Martin is consumed by hopelessness and can't sleep, it repeats comforting words: 'You will succeed, Martin. You will succeed.'

And then, one morning, the big bell tolls, and gaunt figures stumble out of their houses. Their cheeks are hollow, their chests sunken. Their nerves are shattered by the nightly howls of ghosts. And their eyes are dull, deprived of all things beautiful for so long. There has been nothing beautiful to see, what with the fog enveloping the castle courtyard all day long, obscuring any light or view, leading them to believe that all that will remain until the end of time is this muddy courtyard. Their zest for life has faded. Yet now the bell rings, and they gather.

The princess also appears on her balcony, casting her gaze upon the miserable limbo she has created. Oh, how she suffers. The smell from down below. She holds a hand-kerchief to her mouth.

Thomann is there, now just a shadow of his former self. He has shaved his head and can be recognised only by his two-tone trousers. Martin is the first to reach him. Thomann has built something, pieced it together, bit by bit, though at first it's impossible to understand its purpose. He stands tall. He receives his weary and sickly audience in a shirt with ruffled sleeves. With a gesture, he acknowledges the balcony and bows.

'The time has come,' he proclaims proudly. And his voice carries quite far. Where does he find the strength? He probably only needs it one last time.

The horseman remains in the doorway, as do the wife and children.

But the others make their way towards him.

'Yes, come closer. You are the ones I like best. I've spent nights worrying, pondering, goodness knows how, I didn't have much left.'

He grins. Martin wonders where his teeth have gone.

'Yes, our dearest princess.' He waves up to the balcony. She doesn't move. 'She charged me with a tricky task. I was to execute but not kill myself.'

Not everyone understands the difference right away, but that doesn't matter.

Marie joins him. The weeks have not affected her. She is as dishevelled and amiable as ever.

'How nice that you have all come,' she says, and walks among them as if she were holding court.

'Enjoy this,' Thomann calls out, and kisses Marie's hand as he passes. 'I gave it my best shot. Tell your children about it. And your children's children. And your children's children's children, for today Thomann is learning to fly.'

Marie giggles and applauds.

Thomann positions himself in front of a shovel-like board and snaps his fingers, at which the three-eyed goat limps over. It begins to chew on a rope that has been soaked in a liquid. Sugar water. He must have gone without himself to obtain it. Everyone watches. The jester smiles. He no longer looks at Martin. He only sees a comforting emptiness ahead and waits.

No sooner has the goat chewed through the rope than the torn cord triggers a reaction on the scaffolding and among the objects, and this in turn another, and this in turn another. A wealth of lively events begins. A bucket lowers; water spills, driving a wheel; a stone plops into a bowl of red paint, splattering the audience; colourful cloths dance up and down, pink powder tints the fog. Marie claps her hands enthusiastically. And on it goes. Embers ignite and ropes burn, creating the illusion of light purposefully hurrying along them. Balls are set in motion and roll down a pathway; a small grinder, perhaps made from the jester's teeth, grinds a piece of string and while everyone is still astonished and gradually recovering their smiles, an increasingly serene expression spreads across the jester's face. He's almost there, Martin thinks.

The next instant, a stone, large and heavy as a cannonball, crashes down onto a wedge that has been set up, and with a single sweeping movement, the shovel-like board hurls Thomann over the castle wall out into the fog.

Everyone is completely shocked; even time would like to stand still. He learned to fly, Martin thinks, he is dying without us.

For a long time, everyone stares into the empty space where the jester disappeared. They can't believe what has happened. They wait a long time to see if it might have been a jest and Thomann will come crawling back over the wall at any moment, thumbing his nose at them. But he doesn't.

Eventually the princess shrugs her shoulders and makes a move to leave the balcony.

Martin is still staring into the fog, while the others gradually give up waiting for Thomann, longing to return to their desolation. But behold – Martin is the first to see it.

148 · STEFANIE VOR SCHULTE

'Look,' he says quietly. 'Don't you see it?'

Don't you see how the fog is clearing? Did the jester play a good trick? Did he tear a hole in the wall with his flight? Perhaps a hole in time. Don't you see how the sun sparkles behind the mist? A brilliant, glistening day is emerging. Brighter than all the light of the past weeks. And it clears, faster and faster. How splendid the light is. And beautiful. Everyone exclaims with delight. It's probably spring by now. Are the mountains still there? The familiar rocks and gorges and meadows in the surrounding valley? Forests in the distance, blue sky, a world they believed lost. Everyone scrambles for a spot, a view, everyone holds their faces to the wind, smiles at one another, and indeed, they see five horsemen down on the path making their way up the slope.

'The horsemen are coming!' they shout, and they cheer and fall into each other's arms so that the lice get all mixed up.

Only Martin remains motionless. He knows that they have found the children. They are bringing the children to the castle.

The inhabitants are so weakened that they can barely open the gate. The horsemen approach slowly. Everyone waits.

Only Marie remains standing at the wall, looking into the clear sky, wondering where her brother is, and she laughs at how amusing he looked when flying.

The horsemen reach the courtyard. They nod graciously, somewhat taken aback by the haggard faces. Yes, it took them a long time. A few of their attempts failed. One or two abductions did not go smoothly. There were quarrels among the horsemen. Rifts. But eventually, they succeeded. Which cloak conceals the girl? Which one the boy?

However, the horsemen have brought someone else with them. He is seated on the last horse. He is carrying a dirty bundle and when Martin spots him, he recognises him instantly. The painter.

Martin wants to shout out, but a sensation overwhelms him, as if he were drowning in it. No sound at first, but then Martin shouts: 'Painter!' And he longs to run over to him, but his legs refuse to comply. Have they melded with the wretched ground? Has Martin been here for so long that he has become part of the castle, part of this doomed community?

'Painter!' Martin calls once more.

And the man hears him. He sees the boy among all the other figures. He swiftly dismounts and rushes towards the child. He calls his name, hugs him and picks him up. This familiar lightness. This fragile human child. Eyes radiating goodness.

'To find you here!' the painter says, not realising that tears are streaming down his face. Martin smiles. He had never dared to hope that he would see the painter again.

The horsemen observe these events for a bit, then they grow impatient and demand that the painter hurries up.

'The princess is waiting!' they say.

The painter waves them off. 'You know, Martin,' he says, 'I always get the most bizarre commissions.'

'You don't know how right you are,' the child says.

The horsemen call the painter again. Martin is not allowed to accompany them. They push him aside a little. They don't want to share their loot.

But the painter and the boy know that only a castle wall separates them. They are in the same place now.

'I will join you!' Martin shouts to the painter.

'Was that your father?' the wife asks later.

Martin looks at the bread that the princess has had distributed. Bread and apples and a piece of bacon for everyone.

He shakes his head. He had a father. And now it is time.

'Explain the sleep game to me,' Martin says.

28

It takes a few weeks, but by the beginning of spring the villagers show barely any traces of the suffering they endured during the dark time. Traders resume their journeys on the roads. The princess donates animals for breeding, as well as milk and eggs. It is surprising how quickly everyone forgets, how rapidly they recover. The tranquil nights have a healing effect. Strength has been regained for the clean-up, the removal of rubbish. And when life flows smoothly once again, people are given the opportunity to sign up for the sleep game.

Farmers, drovers, burghers come forward to register and present their requests. The winner of the sleep game is allowed to state a wish, which the princess will grant without hesitation, or so they say. However, it's not something you should count on.

A lectern has been set up in front of the castle gate. A scribe and his gofers await those who want to participate. They handle the administration of hope. There is a long line of applicants. Not everyone is allowed through. No drunks, as they tend to cause trouble. No women either, please, they might cause confusion. Whingers who express their despair during the application stage are deemed annoying and turned away.

Never before has a child registered. So there is some confusion when Martin steps forwards.

'What's your name?' the scribe at the wooden lectern asks. There are probably ten men waiting behind Martin.

'Martin.'

'How old are you?'

Martin doesn't know. The experienced scribe scrutinises him closely. The beautiful eyes that carry both pain and innocence. The long, thin limbs.

'Thirteen, fourteen?'

Martin nods. He is so excited that his mouth is dry. The scribe notes down the number.

'And what is your request?' he then asks.

'I want to speak to the princess.'

'Everyone wants that. But what is your request?'

'I want to tell the princess that.'

'But I need to write it down first.'

'Why?' Martin asks.

'So that I can announce it.'

'You mean when I win?'

'If you should win, then I could announce it,' the scribe clarifies, drumming his fingers on the lectern.

'How likely do you think it is that I'll win?' Martin asks.

'Highly unlikely.'

'Then it's completely unnecessary for you to write it down.'

The men behind him grunt in agreement. The scribe sighs.

'You need someone to vouch for you.'

Martin doesn't understand.

'Someone to pay for the damage you might cause during the game. Someone who can guarantee us that your intentions are honourable. Someone who will clean up if you should kill yourself.'

Martin is baffled. What's this all about? The scribe waves his quill pen around.

'I don't know,' Martin says.

'So, no one,' the scribe says, about to dismiss the boy.

'I can vouch for him.' A voice. The horseman's wife. She is dressed in her finest attire. She stands tall and radiates beauty.

'Fair enough,' the scribe says. 'But you are a woman.'

'You are quite astute,' the wife retorts.

'So your vouching for him doesn't count.'

The wife laughs. But the scribe doesn't laugh.

'Seriously?' she asks.

'Women don't count.'

'But the princess is a woman too,' Martin says.

'Don't call her a woman,' the scribe mumbles.

'Then I will vouch,' a voice sounds from afar.

The people make way for the limping horseman. He leans heavily on his stick. And his word counts. But he doesn't sign, claiming he can't write. His wife does so instead and the scribe is offended.

And so Martin is allowed to take part in the sleep game.

29

All those who are permitted to participate are prepared within the castle. White shirts are distributed. Martin puts his on; naturally, it is too big for him. I look like a ghost now, he thinks.

The rules are read out. That does not take long. The objective of the game is to stay awake the longest. Whoever falls asleep is eliminated. You are permitted to eat and drink, talk, play cards and keep busy during the game. The players are closely supervised, under constant observation, and now, good luck.

In the initial twelve hours, the participants watch each other furtively, form partnerships, share stories. Some fool around; perhaps their request is not that important. Maybe they have merely lost a bet. They also talk to Martin. He is given advice. They recommend he give up straight away.

Two individuals fall asleep after twenty-four hours due to excessive eating and drinking. The guards escort them from the hall; all the others are allowed to switch rooms.

Martin's eyes are burning, and he frequently rubs them.

'Are you feeling all right?' the rooster asks.

'I am fine,' says Martin.

'Talk to me. You have to talk to me to stay awake.'

'They will think I am mad,' says Martin, while he continues to think about his father. Now he knows that he must also have worn a shirt like this. Might it even be this very one, which is torn at the cuffs? A patched tear across the chest. Did his father get caught on something with the shirt? Did he also pace back and forth to stay awake? Did he also only sit down when he was doing well or wanted to eat something? Did he also look at the paintings and discover the holes with unceasingly peering eyes? Did he also feel his thoughts beginning to vibrate, with a pain that makes the scalp tingle?

After thirty-six hours everyone starts talking gibberish. There is also laughter. They grow jumpy. And they make a lot of noise, because they can no longer control their movements. A few more fall asleep. They rest their heads on the ice-cold marble sills in front of the window and sleep on their feet.

The guards wake them with a kick to their backside. There is a great deal of shouting as they are forcibly ejected.

Martin incessantly circles around the room's walls. He runs his fingers over the objects until he knows their sequence off by heart.

Again they move to a different room. The next one is full of paintings, each one depicting the princess with her children. Her mocking, severe countenance looks down at the sleep-deprived, who stagger and slur their words and slap each other to stay awake.

The rooster pecks at Martin under his shirt. The boy develops a fever. He drinks copious amounts of water and pours it over his head, which hurts so much that he would like to take it off. The shadows under his eyes are grey. The guards watch him very closely. Yet Martin perseveres, sometimes wishing he wouldn't because gradually a fear he has never known begins to consume him.

'It's not your fear,' the rooster says. 'It's the children's fear.'

A dreadful fear that dwells in the eyes of the children depicted in each of the paintings. Princess with children and dog. Princess with children in a meadow. Princess with children studying books, in splendid robes, playing music, riding. And the children always seem the same, but Martin knows they are always different. He searches the paintings for Godel's daughter, compares the shape of the eyes and the curve of the lips, but he cannot find the girl and at some point he no longer knows what it is that distinguishes the girl from the others. That is the moment he bursts into tears.

'I have forgotten what she looks like,' he sobs.

The children's fear seeps out of the paintings like lead and fills the room, until Martin flees to a chair in horror, from there onto a table and then tries to climb the wall. In the process, his shirt tears at the mended seam, and the sound brings Martin back to his senses.

'Exactly the same,' the rooster says. That's exactly how his father went mad.

When dawn breaks, one of the men hurls himself out of the tower window. Another repeatedly smashes his forehead against the stone wall until blood streams over his eyes.

'That should do it,' he declares triumphantly. And yet he falls asleep immediately.

On the fourth day, Martin's head is on fire and he is having palpitations. He has trouble breathing. Simple tasks that have been second nature all his life now become complex endeavours. It's as if he constantly has to think of taking in air and then expelling it again or else he will suffocate.

'What if I forget that too?' Martin says.

'I will remind you,' the rooster says.

The remaining participants are admitted into the hall of mirrors. There are only three of them left. The guards take pity on the child. It might be the case that one of them doesn't immediately report when Martin blinks for longer than it actually takes to blink. Perhaps there is even one slight nudge against the boy's leg to rouse him from his slumber. Martin is suffering torments.

No one can help him in the hall of mirrors. He is utterly alone here, confronted by his own reflection and a multitude of demons that crowd into his mirror image. How they yearn to chase him out of the distorted reflection of his embattled soul.

'Leave me be,' Martin implores, and yet he has to confront them all anew. The fallen warriors from the war, with their decomposing bodies and hollowed skulls. Dancing

Thomann and his crowned goats. Graceful Gloria with her clapping baby. The dead boy whose body the parents wouldn't give up. He sees Wandering Ulrich, the ghastly fellow. And he imagines the pit where the bodies of the princess's children lie when they have become superfluous and have been replaced. Could there be so many that they fill the mountain upon which the castle stands?

He sees wolves prowling amid the mirrors and hears their jaws sinking into the necks of cranes.

He also sees his father in his white shirt. He sees him waving from a distant night. Silently and desolately existing on the other side of life. And there is the princess, handing his father an axe. Or is it Marie? Or is it Franzi? Is it Seidel or Henning? Who hands the axe to his father, compelling him to return home and kill his own family because of the unyielding grip of nightmare and terror?

The hand. The axe. His father's gaze. Martin hears his own scream mingling with the rooster's crow. He lifts a weighty cup and shatters the mirror with it.

I will make it stop, thinks Martin.

I will put an end to this, he thinks.

I will end it now.

In the next instant, light cascades into the hall of mirrors. A door has opened.

'Come,' a voice beckons. 'You have won. The princess will see you now.'

30

Yes, now he is allowed to see the princess. He has won the sleep game. He can present his request. Save the children.

But he needs to be patient a little while longer.

Martin is waiting outside the grand door, asleep on his feet, and would have fallen had it not been for the guards, who are moved by the pitiful sight of the boy, and so they brace him, left and right, ready to fend off any criticism that might come from the ladies-in-waiting or passing servants. Yet no one reports them and no one says a word, so the boy is able to sleep for a few minutes. Although even the thunderous boom of cannons would probably not have roused him. The rooster rests against the boy's chest; the boy rests against the guard's arm. His exhaustion finds solace in the knowledge that he has succeeded. At least, that is what Martin believes.

Finally, the princess finds time to receive the child. The door opens. Martin wakes up as he is pushed to his feet and ushered into the room.

The chirping of countless songbirds fills the air. They flutter about the room, displaying their vibrant colours and restless energy. They perch on mantelpieces and curtain rails. On the princess's bedposts. Bird droppings everywhere. The floor is carpeted with soft feathers.

The princess assumes her customary pose, supported by pillows. She is coughing more than ever. The baby is in her arms. The children sit on the covers. They are dazed and feeble. They are still unaccustomed to the role forced upon them. They haven't been suffering it for very long – which is why they are suffering terribly.

The painter stands in the corner working on a canvas. What is he painting? Green fields and a picnic blanket. But Martin knows that the children will never again experience the outdoors or the sensation of grass beneath their feet. They only have this year left. But what does the painter know about this? Does he suspect anything? His tension is palpable and his smile, which now reaches Martin, betrays his concern.

Martin's heart aches profoundly.

'Come closer,' the princess says, beckoning. 'Let me look at you.'

He approaches the bed. The princess holds songbirds in her palm and allows them to peck at some grain. When she coughs, the birds briefly take flight, but quickly return.

'A child has never participated before,' she remarks. Her breathing is laboured. Her lungs make a raspy sound when she draws breath, and a wheezing sound when she exhales. Martin feels his own chest tighten.

'You must be exceptionally brave,' she says, and her words are meant to sound friendly, but Martin yearns to flee and stop listening to her.

The rooster is kicking under Martin's shirt. He takes it out and places it on his shoulder.

'The wonderful creature!' the princess exclaims. 'I wonder if it might utter something marvellous again! Something amusing! Something audacious!' Her delight is evident. It is unbearable to see how she rejoices while the girl on the covers collapses in a faint. The little boy straightens her up again. Hastily. Fearful, before the princess notices.

There is the painted lady, clapping her hands. Martin rubs his hands. He must say it now. He is allowed to present his request. The time has come.

'I want to take the children,' Martin says.

Yet the princess only has eyes for the creature. She entices the rooster with grain.

'I want to take the children, do you hear?' Martin repeats.

The painter lowers his brush. Never again will he leave this child.

'Cluck, cluck, cluck,' the princess says to the rooster.

Martin gets fidgety. Why is she not listening to him? Why is she not paying attention to him?

'You have to stop,' he says. A little louder. He barely has any strength left. 'You cannot steal any more children!'

The princess glares at him. 'Why not?' she says. 'I can do as I please.'

'Why not!' Martin shrieks. 'Why are you allowed to do as you please? What you are doing is wrong.'

'But I like it,' she says.

'But you are wrong. You are very wrong.'

The guards exchange glances. Should they intervene? The princess does not seem upset. She seems content and satisfied. The new children are doing well in their new role. It has only taken a few blows. They also cried much less than the others. It hasn't even been necessary to show them the view from the bell tower. It is going to be a good year. A good year with little children whom she loves so much. She feels young and strong. She will live forever and remain beautiful forever. It is so good to feel herself again. All the happiness of youth is flowing through her body. She will be a good princess this year. Wise and clever. Such a pity that the jester has gone. Where might she find a replacement? At least she has a painter. She is happy with him. And of course she will take the rooster. Perhaps it can crow compliments. She would like it to perch on the tower in the mornings, praising the princess's beauty. Yes, but there is the matter of the boy.

What is it that the boy wants? Why is he so upset? He is quite flushed.

'She is not listening,' the rooster says.

'Ah, look,' the princess calls out delightedly. 'It is doing it again.'

'Give me the children,' Martin says.

'Of course not,' the princess says.

'You must,' the rooster says. 'You must give them to him. And you must never steal any ever again.'

The princess laughs at him. 'And your second wish?' she finally asks. She doesn't want to take too narrow a view today.

'There is no second wish,' Martin says. He says it very quietly. His ears are hurting and his heart is stumbling around in his chest as if it were looking for the way out. He feels as fragile and tremulous as a songbird, whereas just moments ago, when he entered the room, he thought he was a horseman, a gaunt hero, a child capable of riding and healing. All that seems lost now. The princess is not listening, and it is no different to sitting in his village talking to Henning, Sattler and Seidel. No one listens and no one keeps their promises.

It may be that the princess did grant and fulfil the wish of one or two winners of the sleep game. She is even said to have given fields as presents. Well, strictly speaking, she took the fields away from someone and then gave them to someone else; what does she care about the devastation this causes the original owners? Those without fields are left with no income and nothing to eat. They must still feed children and elderly grandparents, who will throw themselves off the hayloft so as not to be a burden. Which worked for the grandmother at her first attempt. Not for the grandfather. He just broke his leg and shoulder and groaned his way up the ladder to the hayloft again and threw himself down, head first this time. That time it worked. But what does the princess know about such hardships? She sits there coughing and wheezing amid her songbirds, her stolen children.

'It is not yet done,' the rooster says. He says it into Martin's wounded heart. 'Just one more time,' the creature says.

I can't go on, Martin thinks. Everything in me is old and lived, long past and worn out. Now I am here and I can't bear another thought, another delay, another setback. She is not going to give me the children.

'It is not this moment that must count,' the rooster says.

The painter has long since set down his brushes and paints and forgotten about them. How can he help? My God, the boy is dying before my eyes, he thinks.

The songbirds are darting and swooping madly around them. Their incessant twittering gets under Martin's skin, gnawing at his bones. The feathers. The cranes' calls. The princess's eye, milky with age, which is supposed to serve as the gateway to a soul. Yet, upon closer inspection, there is nothing within – only pale wax and a feverish self, woven into the everlasting cough.

And of course Martin cannot know yet what will become known later. But he can and does see beyond his lack of education and the ignorance of his century, sees the fever that is weakening the princess and hears the rattling coming from her body, from the clogged-up and useless branches of her lungs. He senses the harm that emanates from the lead white on her skin. How it gradually seeps into her body. How she licks the dry traces from her lips. Her abdomen aches. She is lying down. Her chamber pot has remained empty for days. Then there is the musty odour coming from her bed. Does she even detect the stench? The dust between the birds' feathers. The droppings. All of it is making her sick. Inflaming her body. Each flutter of wings in that room is a step towards death. And Martin might have thought that he had done everything, given everything, but there is one more thing he must do. It is just a few strides to the bed.

He tenderly and slowly strokes his beloved rooster, the rhythm matching the unhurried pace of his steps towards the bed.

Dearest friend, Martin thinks.

The time has come, the rooster's voice in his head says.

Martin reaches the princess and places the rooster on the frail chest of this witch, this tyrant, this murderess, and the rooster begins a frenzied dance on top of her, clutching tightly and flapping its wings, raising clouds of dust and dirt. The princess screeches, ingesting the dirt. The very particles that foretold her demise. Still, everything seems to happen slowly. Martin reaches the little boy, the eight-year-old, barely taller than a child of five, and lifts him onto his back. The little boy has wet himself. They will sort it out later.

'Hold on tight,' Martin says to the child.

The rooster also holds on tight and remains on the princess's chest. The painter abandons his paints, brushes and stool and picks up the little girl. She is so drugged that she can barely open her eyes.

No one will stop them while the princess is dying.

Martin, the painter and the children hurry through the corridors and halls. More and more servants are coming towards them. The state of the princess is making the castle tremble. Everyone, everyone suddenly knows about it, as if the parakeets or the paintings on the walls had alerted them. The first arrivals rush to their mistress's bedside – they want to help, or feel they must. But they stop as soon as they behold the ghostly spectacle – the princess's discoloured face and the way her veins strain at her neck. How the rooster's claws tear her clothes. Feathers are raining down from the pillows like snow.

Dead. Let her finally be dead, it flashes through the minds of the ladies-in-waiting. Wouldn't that be something? If she were gone and there was no heir? Then they would have tales to tell. That they witnessed the final spasms. And that no one shed a tear. And that no one wanted to bury her. Which is why they dragged her stiff, cumbersome body to the very shaft where countless children suffered and perished year after year. So there she goes now. There she shall be haunted and consumed by the dead.

Martin and the painter reach the castle courtyard, where everyone has gathered, as if those down below have already sensed that something is coming to an end. Perhaps the villagers believe that they felt a tremor in the mountain, a rumbling that foreshadowed the collapse. But it won't be made easy for them. They won't be swept away to die. They will have to live with what has been, and with what lies ahead. And Martin will have to bear the fact that there can be no farewell, because between him and the others, whether it be the horseman, his wife, perhaps even Marie, stands the knowledge of the rescued children, the awareness of their suffering. He has to suppress the longing to hug the wife. But it is no longer bearable.

And the others do nothing. They remain motionless. The shame. The shame. Henceforth, they will have to deal with it, and denial will offer little solace.

The rooster flutters out of the tower window, seeking rest under Martin's shirt after its repugnant exertions. Martin keeps it safe.

Might it be a coincidence that the horseman's horse stands at the castle gate? There is a blanket on it, in any case, as well as a sack of provisions. Martin lifts the boy onto the animal. The painter places the girl alongside. They lead the animal out of the castle. Away from the court. Down the mountain. And into the valley.

31

The worst is over, but it takes time to recover, and they fear setbacks. Martin dreams and startles from his sleep at night, and it takes a long time for him to feel calm in the face of the dark shadows in the forest they roam through on their journey. The mountainous limestone terrain soon shifts to the muddy ground of drenched meadows.

At first there is no knowing where the children come from. Their descriptions of their home villages sound like the descriptions of any other village that might be home to a child. They know all about cows and goats, the slingshot of the boy next door, and the priest's bad habits, but nothing about the next town or the view from the top of the hill.

The painter makes a rough map on which he notes the areas they have travelled through since leaving the castle. They mark the places they have already searched, and finally they come upon a landscape that looks familiar to one of the children.

It is the boy whom they bring home, to his parents' humble door. The mother takes the child in her arms, so

very tightly that it seems she might crush him. The grati-
tude in her eyes is enough for Martin, and that is all the
thanks that can be offered. After all, he snatched the children from the devil, came close to him, fought him. No one
will be able to face him without a shudder. So he moves on
quickly, to find the home of the little girl, in whose face
Martin still recognises Godel's daughter. In his dreams he
apologises to her for not being able to save her. But instead
he has saved all the children who are and will be as she
once was.

'I am so tired,' Martin says sometimes. And it doesn't
really matter whether he says it to the rooster or to the
painter.

The man tries to steer the horse and leads them across
sandy forest floors and through small streams.

'There is so much I remember,' Martin says.

'You are still a child,' the painter says.

'I can't bear any more.'

'It will be different from now on,' the rooster says.

'Will it?'

'You may rest now. You may hope. You may wish.'

'What does that mean?' Martin asks.

The rooster doesn't reply, and the painter doesn't know.
The boy remains silent for a long time. And it is true. He
did once wish for something. It was always there, simply
there, growing inside him over time like a faint, everlasting light. But then it was gradually stifled by all his deeds,
because he had to achieve fulfilment through his task.
And now there will be room again for this wish that lies

hidden within him. Martin feels the gentle tug and begins to uncover the wish, little by little. And often he sits by the fire, staring into space with his large eyes, unresponsive, while sparks from the firewood fly up to the sky.

Then they find the little girl's home, and Martin seems to recognise the area too.

Her mother can hardly believe that she has got her daughter back. She falls to the ground crying. A long time passes before she can even take the child in her arms. Anyone not moved to tears must already be dead.

As thanks they are given provisions. Martin and the painter move on. Now they have space on the horse. Perhaps they will sell it and buy paints for the painter. Or a home.

As the weather gets warmer, they rest by a river. Martin bathes in it, while the painter sits on the riverbank; having a wash is the furthest thing from his mind. Instead, he imagines painting what he sees: the edge of the forest in the background; blue sky above and white clouds, finely flecked like feathers. Martin suddenly shouts out and pulls his head out of the water.

'Franzi!' he shouts.

He longs to see her again! She should come with them! They should return to the village once more. Back to where it all began.

'Have you thought about it properly?' the painter asks.

'No, not at all,' Martin says.

The boy beams. He can light up the darkest hour with his smile. His nature is so pure, his hope for happiness so bright.

With Franzi's image before him, everything feels easy to the boy. He slips into his shirt and trousers, still wet, and urges the painter to set off.

The painter does not see the need to hurry. He wants to advise the child not to try it, not to enter the village ever again. Wasn't that once the plan? The people are loathsome. And meanwhile Franzi, this nimble spirit, born into the wrong time, has probably been taught what she should be like: pretty but not blooming. Strong, but more like a workhorse. Cunning, but only to talk others out of their last coin and gain an advantage. But not clever.

As the painter contemplates the situation, he realises something. Franzi and the boy: my God, they could turn the world upside down. It would do the world good for once. If only all the wretched people could then plunge into the heavens. Oh. This gives the painter an idea for a painting. He grows still and sees it before him: a painting that does not show the fall of the angels or the ascension of Jesus, but humanity taking off into the clouds. As if they were being torn away, eyes wide in terror and limbs wildly twisted, so that earth would remain for the good ones. How beautiful it would be if, for once, the rivers were not full of blood and the fish did not float in them belly-up. If the fields could flourish without being places of clandestine desecration, without the newly sprouting plants having to find their way to the light through clothes torn from limbs. It would be peaceful and, perhaps, even a little dull. Perhaps even so dull that the painter might run out of ideas in the long run. And he wonders whether he could live with that, if there were no longer anything cruel to be painted in colour on canvas. Then he would probably paint the boy forever. Just him, and he wouldn't need any other colour except gold to do so.

Martin has only passed through this area once before. When he left. A long time ago. Yet every stone seems familiar to him. He feels something clench inside him. Unsure what to call it, he asks the painter.

'Anticipation,' the painter says. 'You call that anticipation.'

That makes sense to Martin because he is so looking forward to seeing Franzi and taking her with him. It doesn't even occur to him that she might not want to or might no longer be there.

'You know she could also be dead,' the painter says.

'That's not like her,' Martin says.

'She might have got married. Perhaps she has children.'

'I like children,' Martin says.

'It probably won't be that simple.'

'It will be much simpler,' Martin says.

'Christ.' It slips from the painter's mouth. He is afraid that Martin will be disappointed. He has achieved so much already. If only he didn't have to torture himself any more.

'Never mind,' the painter says, and they ride during the day and sleep under the open sky.

At one point, they ride through a field of ash and realise too late that it is the ashes of countless dead that puff up like powder beneath the horse's hooves. No matter how slowly they make the animal walk, the ashes swirl up and settle like a grey veil on their skin and hair, and they trail grey clouds of dust behind them that must surely be visible from the other side of the earth. Ash sticks to their nostrils and parches their throats. They have to spit and blow their noses. Later they find a stream and rinse the dead off their skin, avoiding any mention of the bones and skulls that lay scattered in the middle of the ash desert.

Gradually they grow accustomed to the horse. They let it graze and are happy when it carries them for a while. Franzi would enjoy riding on it, Martin thinks.

During these days, they encounter no one. It is not far now, the boy knows. It cannot be far now. They traverse the next piece of forest, the hill they are riding towards, the path leading down. Martin recognises the way. This is where he saw the horseman and followed him; this is where the black horse reared up as Martin tried to catch up with him, Godel's daughter hidden beneath the horseman's cloak. The force of the memory makes the boy grow pale.

They finally reach the village. The boy does not rejoice but is immensely excited. He spots smoke curling out of the chimneys. Well, well, everyone still seems to be here. The painter grits his teeth and wishes he could have stopped Martin, but the boy, undaunted, leads the horse along the road until they reach the square. The well, the church gate, the rose hips and there, in the shade of a tree, the eternal triad, Henning, Seidel and Sattler, playing cards at a little table on stones and chairs. They call out what they have, announcing their tricks. They raise and lower their hands, picking up cards from the table. The cards are dealt again, and the po-faced men look at their cards that they then press closely to their chests. They chew on their lips; Seidel snorts blood from his encrusted nose. When Martin and the painter come closer, they can see that the men bear wounds. Blue-rimmed cheeks, bruises, a swollen eye, burst lower lips, torn shirtsleeves – what has happened here?

Martin leaves the horse by the well. He gazes longingly at the tavern. Will Franzi still be there? A cat wanders past. Shadows appear behind windows.

The three men play on until the painter and Martin approach. The painter asks: 'What are you playing to win?'

A pig or a chicken, honour – if they have any or think they do – or a jug of schnapps, what are they likely to be playing for?

The three don't answer at first; they are too busy staring in astonishment. The dratted child is back again. No, no longer a child. Big and angular in the face. The kind eyes. Damn, why is he even still alive?

'You!' blurts out Henning. And of course he means both of them. The painter who botched their altarpiece and the boy who ruined their self-satisfaction.

Martin greets them. Seidel blinks; Sattler gives a little cough and holds his fractured rib.

'What do you think?' Henning finally says. 'Up here, what is there to play for?'

'Franzi,' Martin says.

'Damned boy,' Seidel says.

'I want to take her,' says Martin.

'What is he talking about?' says Sattler.

'Franzi,' repeats Martin.

'Yes,' says Henning. 'We are talking about Franzi.'

'What a bint.'

'You are playing for Franzi?' the painter probes.

'Yes, of course.'

'I'm going to go and fetch her,' Martin says calmly.

'You will not.'

'But I want to take her with me.'

'Well, you'll have to ask her first,' Seidel says.

'Just like you are asking her if you can play to win her?' Martin asks.

That shuts them up for a while as they shuffle the newly stacked cards.

'If we played properly here, Franzi would long be mine,' Henning grunts after a while. 'But the bastards here cheat as if the aces were growing out of their ears.'

'Who cheats?' Seidel asks.

'And who is the bastard?' Sattler asks.

They quickly become embroiled in an argument.

You might wonder how long this has been going on. Whether they have been vying for Franzi's affections for years or just weeks, every game ends in a quarrel, which is why they never get a result and all three remain losers – which is how they appear to Martin and the painter anyway.

There is a blow to the nose, an ugly crunching sound; Sattler howls, and blood sprays over his shirt and hand.

'Marvellous way of handling things,' the painter says. 'And where is Franzi?'

'In the church,' Seidel gasps from Sattler's headlock.

Martin immediately turns and heads for the church. Henning also jumps up right away. Sattler promptly lets go of Seidel, who comes along too, of course. They shove their way past Martin and all try and make their way through the modest door, pleasing to the Lord, at the same time.

The interior is dark and musty. Neglected too. Leaves have blown in and never been swept away. Birch dust from the spring still sticks to the benches and backrests.

An unfathomable coolness dwells in the walls and evokes in Martin memories of his own existence, as if they needed to be summoned. And these also include those memories that should actually be inaccessible to him, because he was too young.

How he was baptised in this church. A brief and modest occasion, but he'd been held by smiling people. His mother's hard, worn hands, still warm, and her long hair on his face in the evenings, when she tried combing it while nursing the little boy at the same time. Happiness resided here. His father's humming to soothe him. For he cried. He cried so much that it was as though he could already foresee his fate and was inconsolable about it. As if he were lamenting the boy he had to become. The boy whose feet are full of blisters, whose body is covered in wounds, while the little infant himself remains untouched and soft. Fresh and pure amidst the chaos of the little hut, where scolding and laughter coexist, where soup is steaming and the next day they go hungry again. Where he receives kisses from his siblings. And his crying only ends when his mother uses the broom to shoo a cheeky fox away from the chickens, instead placing the baby on the sandy floor, among the grain, where the rooster finds him.

The creature struts around the child, they gaze at one another, and at this moment, Martin stops crying and doesn't grumble or cry again. His eyes are curious now, big and beautiful. Everything can rest in them now, as they are forever focused on the black creature. And likewise, the creature only has eyes for the child, restless unless it is by Martin's side. From then on, they are inseparable and completely at peace with each other. Father just shrugs his shoulders. So what, he thinks, it's a rooster and people talk. The child is content. So be it.

Martin now places his hand on the rooster, his faithful friend. The memories fade again; a figure is sitting at the front of the church, looking at the altarpiece that the villagers hate. Franzi, on the other hand, loves it. The picture that shows Martin's mild expression on the face of the crucified. And it is she who sits there at the front.

She turns around when she hears the commotion at the door, unafraid of the three men who are playing for her as if she has no reason or right to object. She catches sight of the boy and her face lights up. Pure love.

She would have liked to run to him. But she knows that they will have plenty of time to embrace one another. They will have time for the rest of their lives. She assesses the situation perfectly. It is always the same. The back and forth when they enter the church, the eternal quarrel because the three idiots can't fit through the door that pleases the Lord.

The three of them are truly exasperated. Might Martin, who has travelled so far, not have some advice for them? If they are honest, they would like their old church door back. This brings them back to the question of the key, and to the deliberations about the use of violence to the door, which has long been consecrated by the installation of a second door.

'Where is Hansen?' Martin asks. He asks very calmly.

They exchange glances, struggling to recall.

Martin jogs their memory. 'Mad Hansen, the organ player.'

'Well, he's dead,' is the reply.

'That's a pity,' Martin says. 'And how was he buried?'

'Well, lying down,' comes the reply.

'No,' Martin says. 'In what clothes? Was he wearing a shroud? Or was he wearing his normal clothes?' Hansen's jacket, the one he always wore. Red, with faded ribbons.

The men exchange glances.

'He didn't have a shroud. How could he? With a screw loose, he couldn't find a wife to sew or stitch.'

'What a miracle that you managed to find one,' Franzi says. Martin loves her very much.

It is shocking to see how much the village has deteriorated. There is no priest and no undertaker, which is why Henning, Seidel and Sattler make all the important decisions, which sooner or later will destroy the village – that much is for certain. All three of them are very conceited, which also makes them extremely dim-witted, mean and self-important, with limited intelligence. They mostly conduct funerals from memory, which results in various oversights. You can count yourself lucky that the bodies even make it into the coffins. In any case, Hansen was buried in his jacket. Ah.

'Fine,' says Martin. 'Then you'll have to dig him up and look for the key in his jacket.'

The others are perplexed. And this pleases Martin.

'Don't you remember?' he asks, and reminds them of the day of the thunderstorm, when the painter arrived, the key had disappeared and Martin went to see the priest. 'The door was locked, but Hansen was inside.' He must have locked the door from the inside. What else could it have been?

The painter laughs. This boy! It is hilarious.

'You are lying,' says Henning, but he can clearly recall, although he would rather not know, how Hansen had staggered towards him. And even Henning now comes to understand that Hansen had been inside, and how could he have locked the door without a key? Damn. Why hadn't they realised that? He knows that Martin is clever. But are they really that stupid?

The realisation seeps into their feet as they scrape the floor uneasily.

'You can check,' Martin says. 'If you can't agree who gets to enter the church first, then you need a bigger door. And you have a bigger door. And Hansen has the key in his jacket.'

'Why didn't you tell us this earlier?' Seidel asks.

'I am just a boy,' says Martin. 'What do I know?'

'And how are we supposed to get our hands on the key now?'

'Well, you'll have to dig Hansen up,' says Martin. Franzi's eyes widen.

The three men stand rigidly, and it is the same as it always is when something suddenly pauses which is usually utterly constant and always in motion. Something else emerges from the stillness and becomes entirely obvious.

How idle the evening birdsong sounds. How the cows bellow in the fields because Drefs is such a terrible milker that half the cows go unmilked and the animals almost go mad from the pain of their overfull udders. In between, you can hear the dry rustling in the trees. The mice scurry through the branches of the bushes. And the scent. The wonderful smell of damp earth. Of Franzi's skin.

Martin has never been close enough to know it. But the scent – quite distinct from everything else – that must be her scent.

Martin reaches for Franzi's hand. Her fingers immediately nestle into his as if they had never done anything else. Now is the time, he thinks, and knows that the rooster thinks the same, and so they leave.

Martin doesn't even need to ask Franzi or pull her hand. As soon as he has the thought, she turns and goes with him. She does not hesitate. The painter also turns. And so they leave.

And they will never know whether the three men dug up poor Hansen and found the key. Or whether to this day they are still arguing about whether they should do it, or whether they should play to determine who digs up Hansen. And if you could look into the future, you could divine the three of them as scrawny old men, tanned by meanness, still holding forth and playing cards, until they no longer know what they are playing for. And one day they will probably hold their noses in the air and remember the man who bore the cross for everyone in the village, who asked the princess what the situation was with the taxes during the years of famine, and who tried to stand up for the villagers, and who lost and went mad in the process and murdered his wife and children, all except for the youngest son. And they, the three men, did not take in his child. But these thoughts will come only briefly and warm their ears, before they quickly forget them again.

And sometimes they will think of the clever child. And then, at some point, they will stop thinking altogether. And when the deck of cards has yellowed, they will play with pieces of bark. And when the first one falls off his chair, dead, the others will barely notice, and at some point they will all be dead, while the villagers have all left or perhaps been taken by the plague, who can know these things.

But Martin, he ventures into the countryside. And every green meadow is his future. Every blooming field is a greeting on his path. He goes into the hazy blue of the hills, which are imprinted on the painter's soul, so that he will still be able to paint their oscillations and crests on his deathbed. Above it all, the hawks call out brightly against a blank sky. The warm sun will gradually warm the rooster's feathers. And inside Martin deliverance resonates like a song. They have suffered enough. They have tasted the bitterness of suffering and the emptiness of hunger. They have built their shelter from the cold, covered one another in tears; their evening lullaby was the sound of screaming.

But now they dream as if it were a life. The meadows stretch like a sea of green all the way to the horizon, across which the evening sun ignites a brilliant band of light. Martin and Franzi are free to dream a life together now, in which they love and respect each other. The painter too. The rooster. Sometimes one of them will awaken within the dream, their face contorted with pain. In these moments, the other will hold them, caress them and draw them back into an embrace, whispering words, guiding them into a calmer place where they can step without needing solid ground under their feet. They have discovered their path, which they now tread together.

And they never let each other go.

ACKNOWLEDGEMENTS

I would like to thank my agent, Caterina Schäfer, for her unswerving confidence and commitment to finding the right publishers for this book.

I thank my children for all the beloved days and nights that I get to spend with them.

And Christian, thank you for all the happiness.

Transforming a manuscript into the book you hold in your hands is a group project.

Stefanie vor Schulte and Alexandra Roesch would like to thank everyone who helped to publish *Boy with a Black Rooster* in English:

THE INDIGO PRESS TEAM

Susie Nicklin
Phoebe Barker
Michelle O'Neill

JACKET DESIGN

Luke Bird

PUBLICITY

Jordan Taylor-Jones

EDITORIAL PRODUCTION

Tetragon
Gesche Ipsen
Sarah Terry

THE
INDIGO
PRESS

The Indigo Press is an independent publisher of contemporary fiction and non-fiction, based in London. Guided by a spirit of internationalism, feminism and social justice, we publish books to make readers see the world afresh, question their behaviour and beliefs, and imagine a better future.

Browse our books and sign up to our newsletter for special offers and discounts:

theindigopress.com

Follow *The Indigo Press* on social media for the latest news, events and more:

🅧 @PressIndigoThe
🅞 @TheIndigoPress
🅕 @TheIndigoPress
🅞 The Indigo Press
🅙 @theindigopress